STARLIGHTS GLEAMING

THE STORY OF JEREMY FLYNN

This story is partly fiction and partly true. It reflects my own journey towards spiritual awakening, with the intention to entertain, inspire, and teach. Through hardship, doubt, and unexpected grace, Jeremy gradually discovers a fragile peace and a new way of walking through life, even as darkening storm clouds gather on the horizon. Yet what awaits him next lies far beyond anything his imagination could fathom.

I invite readers to explore the wonders that shape our world—and the deeper truths that shape us.......Al Fike

INTRODUCTIONS

"This book tells the story of Jeremy Flynn, an ordinary man leading a quiet, solitary life in Central Oregon, whose world is suddenly and irrevocably expanded by an encounter with an extraterrestrial being named Orion. What follows is not a tale of invasion or dystopia, but one of invitation and revelation. Reluctantly at first, and then with the help of the intuitive Sadie Jenkins, Jeremy agrees to become a channel for a message intended for all of humanity.

Starlights Gleaming stands apart in its genre. While many stories of this nature explore the 'what ifs' of alien existence through the lens of conflict or conquest, this narrative centers on hope and profound spiritual truth.

The power of this book lies in its ability to blend a relatable, human story with a universe-spanning message. It challenges us to look beyond our immediate world and consider a higher calling — to live in harmony with the universe.

The journey that Jeremy and Sadie embark upon offers a light that is both illuminating and deeply transformative. Open these pages, and open your mind to a message that may well change your perspective on everything."

Jimbeau Walsh

Celestial Medium, Composer, Author.

—Jimbeau Walsh, Celestial Medium, Composer, Author

ACKNOWLEDGEMENTS

From the Author:

Many thanks go to the number of individuals who helped me to get this book published. I especially want to thank my wife, Jeanne, for all her support as I struggled through the writing process; my editor, Linda Hostettler, who encouraged and refined my writing; and many friends who encouraged and supported me on this road.

Thank you all for helping me to bring this story into print.

Al Fike

December 9 2025

Cover design, graphic art, and content editing

by Linda Hostettler, Design Pro, LLC.

Chapter 1

MADISON

The Willamette Valley in central Oregon was full of small towns servicing the burgeoning agricultural industry that is the valley's life ¬blood. Madison was different. Situated in a sweet spot between the Willamette River and Mount Edison, its juxtaposition to the valley bottom and the impressive peak of the mountain gave it an aura of mystery combined with bucolic beauty. Its location made it a popular spot with tourists and serious climbers. The mountain beckoned many because from the top of its gentle rise a tusk of vertical rock protruded boldly toward the sky. The pinnacle rose up to almost 600 feet, remnants of a long extinct volcano. Considered one of the top ten climbs in the continental US, rock-jocs from all over the world flocked there to test their metal. Some even died trying, but once they glimpsed the improbable verticality of its peak, they were hooked.

Madison made a good living providing services to those brave souls who challenged the mountain. It was a pretty town, established in the late 1800's. It's Victorian and Edwardian homes and buildings gave Madison an air of old-world sophistication. The dappled light of its mature trees lining the streets beckoned many to stroll down its avenues. Boutique hotels, augmented by backpacker hostels, crammed the downtown, and in the summer months it was a tourist mecca.

The people of Madison were friendly, and many had made it their home for decades. Though tourism was its present sweetheart, the town had gone through many iterations over its storied history. The town was the brainchild of James 'Rorry' Madison, a wealthy railway tycoon who chose to sink his millions into the place. Beguiled by its beauty, he was determined to make Madison the new San Francisco of the Northwest. He brought the east/west rail line through. He became Madison's first mayor and tireless promoter. His efforts eventually brought prosperity, though not the way he had envisioned. Taking time to become established in its own time and way, for Madison eventually became a desirable place for enough souls to settle and make it the town it is today. Beautiful stately homes sprung up, industry in the form of logging, and agriculture brought a measure of wealth and stability. Rorry built a grand mansion for himself and family as well as a hotel with impressive views of the mountain. The clever entrepreneur's cash incentives for new homes and businesses contributed to Madison's fast growth. Agriculture had always been the town's mainstay but some industry also contributed to its prosperity. The abundance of rich soil and mild climate made it ideal for growing all manner of fruits and vegetables, as well as an abundance of roses, adding to the region's prosperity and beauty.

For a hundred years, Madison grew and earned its place on the map. Not only for new families wanting to take advantage of its many opportunities, it was also a haven for older people seeking retirement in a mid-sized community that boasted a congenial lifestyle without the inconvenience of living in the big cities north and south of the region.

The main street of Madison was populated by fine restaurants, art galleries, bakeries, boutiques, and antique shops. Many artists and writers made it home, inspired by its charms and low cost of living. Stately buildings fanned out from the courthouse and center square which anchored the town. People of Madison took pride in their town loving the hometown familiarity that it possessed. Residents knew one another and most were tolerant towards their fellow citizens, resolving any conflicts that might arise without much hardship. Harmony prevailed there as a result of its stable population and beautiful setting. People were abundantly friendly and helpful to all. Few places in the region could boast so many parks and pleasure palaces than Madison. Having the oldest movie theater this side of San Francisco, its eye-popping marquee and grand entrance was the most photographed feature of the town. At night its many lights offered a dazzling display for the onlooker. Its interior was equally impressive with the original Art Deco style fully intact from the 40's. The town's visual delights were like a dream from the past, a walk down memory lane that continued to draw folks to its charming ways.

Because of its unique charms, Madison had earned the enviable reputation of being the best small town to live in west of the Rockies. Featured in magazines and newspapers, many flocked there to take in its ambience and beauty. Though its small-town character were fast evolving into something reflecting a modern approach to living, Madison held on to its traditions and remained its bucolic self despite those wishing to make over the town into something more agreeable to prevailing economic forces. The town was stubborn in that way and so it remained a haven of beauty and peace.

Chapter 2

FINDING HOME

Judy Flynn, a single mom, made a big decision to leave her LA home and venture to Madison. Judy was a bit of a dreamer, constantly seeing the grass as greener on the other side. This made her restless. She grew up in a small town and since meeting and marrying the first man that piqued her interest while attending SoCal University, she felt stifled in the big city of LA where they settled. She became a librarian and teacher of literature. Her first love was books. Although when she gave birth to her daughter Megan and soon after, a son Jeremy, there was little time for her passion. She found work in the local high school as more babysitting than true teaching. Her husband, Tom, was becoming ever more distant and she was desperately unhappy. Eventually things came to a boil and the two split.

Seeking to start a new life, she saw an article on Madison in some magazine. It seemed like heaven to her so she pulled up stakes and moved there. She was fortunate to find a job teaching Literature and running the school library in the town's only high school. The teacher before her had finally retired so Judy's timing was perfect. It had seemed that the stars were aligned for her and the kids. She found a fine craftsman-style home on a peaceful, leafy street within her price range, and so her family adventure began. It was a match made in heaven for Judy. But her children, Megan and Jeremy were somewhat hesitant after so many big changes in their early lives.

Megan and her younger brother were born and bred in the city. Moving to a place like Madison seemed daunting and a little scary. Jeremy was the more sensitive child of the two. He lived in his own world, bereft of friends and extremely shy. Megan, however, was the opposite, outgoing and confident. Popular at her junior high school, she was reluctant to lose her friends and start anew in what she perceived as a dorky little town in Oregon.

When they lived in LA, Judy was employed as a teacher in Megan's school. She disliked the cruelty and competitiveness of high school culture. She especially worried about Jeremy entering into that environment. She had been called into Jeremy's school office several times because he was being bullied by the other students. Jeremy didn't seem to have any fight in him, becoming an easy target. When she imagined what high school would look like for her dear son, she shuddered at the thought. Moving to a smaller town offered some solutions to this dilemma and though Jeremy was reluctant, she knew that this would be for the better.

Upon arriving in Madison, Megan had no trouble finding new friends, being the cool kid from LA, but the greatest challenge for an introvert like Jeremy was to open up to strangers. He was a sensitive boy who possessed keen observational skills and a curiosity about the natural world. Jeremy eventually found himself enjoying the freedom that a small town affords. He loved going out into the forest, enjoying the wildlife, streams and mountains, inviting him to challenge his hiking skills and ability to observe everything around him. He would often spy on the other kids in the neighborhood, those he was reluctant to befriend. As a loner, he cultivated a strong independent streak that gave him a sense of who he was and what he wanted early in life. These strengths only grew with time and served him well as he matured. Not one to follow the crowd, he saw things quite differently from his peers. Although not inclined to share his views with others, he became a bit of a rebel, dancing to the beat of a different drummer but outwardly quiet and ever observant. His lone wolf behavior worried his mother and older sister but no amount of coaxing him out of his shell would have the desired effect. At such an early age, he was a confirmed loner, and this would not change for the rest of his life.

Nothing came easy for Jeremy — no obvious personal gifts that would indicate a flowering of youth. His face became riddled with acne and he developed a bit of a stutter. He was a mess; not that such machinations of growing up were unique to him, but because of his acute sensitivity, they were deeply felt. He was not one to brush off those emotional peccadillos and perceived slights coming from his peers.

His mind was obsessed with all the details of difficult encounters with others. Deep within him was a yearning to be liked but he felt that it was a futile effort. Hurt upon hurt brought internal pain that was, at times, unbearable. As he matured, he learned to overcome these challenges and settled into what became a livable life.

As Jeremy grew up, he was destined to become a one-man show. Having picked up various skills as a young man, he eventually settled into self-employment as a gardener/handyman. He liked his work and it afforded him a good but modest living. The majority of his business catered to widows and young families who had little time to keep up with needed chores around the house. He never missed an appointment with a client, as he was fond of calling them, and over the years had cultivated a steady clientele.

Although Jeremy's shyness caused him to be reluctant to communicate and be vulnerable with others, most people perceived him as a calm young man with a somewhat distant demeanor. He was not one to ask for help or in need of much company. Judy worried about his future, which apparently was going to be a singular one and seemingly void of much joy. His ever-present mask of stern resolve confirmed her suspicions that her son was a very unhappy young man.

In some respects, she was right, but Jeremy was satisfied with his life and the companionship he shared with his dog, Rex. Rex was an Australian Cattle Dog who displayed loyalty and slavish dedication to his master, a friendship he had yet to find with his fellow humans. Rex was a compact and muscular breed well known for their stamina and agility. The dog possessed an innate intelligence that fostered a unique bond between them. He knew every nuance of Jeremy's body language and reacted in sync with what Jeremy needed. They were simpatico and inseparable. Rex had a good ear and gave sympathetic nods affirming his appreciation of his master's moods and thoughts. Their internal communication offered the same nourishment one would find in a good conversation with a best friend In Jeremy's mind, what Rex provided in love and companionship was all that he needed.

Jeremy's love life was almost non-existent. . He had a few flings in his last year of high school, but they always resulted in girls seeking better prospects. He was of average height and build, with a somewhat rounded face, straight nose, and blue-grey eyes. Though Jeremy was attractive yet reserved, he preferred to be single. At times he longed for a special girl, but past experiences made him reluctant to date. His mother and sister were determined to correct this situation, but most attempts led to a less than enthusiastic response. Jeremy knew he needed to make a better effort, but he saw it as too much of a bother. Much to the chagrin of his mother and sister, Jeremy was resigned to live a solitary life since women only confused and confounded him.

He liked routine and his chosen career was perfect for Jeremy. He didn't want the stress or boredom of an indoor job, stifled by four walls and incessant sameness. No, what he did afforded him something different every day and he loved it. In many respects, Jeremy's clients were his friends. He enjoyed the daily chit-chats and the usual pleasantries. It fulfilled his need for connection and conversation. His bevy of elderly women were all too happy to spend time over a cup of tea in idle conversation. It was a reflection of the easygoing atmosphere of small-town life with all its charms. There were times, however, when he felt frustrated by their meddling in his personal life and unwelcome suggestions on how to do his job.

Generally, his preferred clients were sweet and motherly. Most of the work that was a part of his daily routine was uncomplicated and easily accomplished. With his truck full of all manner of tools and equipment, tackling most jobs was not onerous. When the weather turned wet and cold, he would busy himself with indoor painting and small renovations. He liked working in the garden most of all. Fresh air, sunshine and the opportunity to work with plants and flowers always fascinated him. He learned many of these skills from the advice given to him by his ladies who had been gardening most of their lives. "Make sure you put that wood ash from the fireplace onto the peonies," was a typical bit of advice proffered by a client. "Add lots of lime and some bone meal to the Clematis so they will thrive." There was enough shared common wisdom that one could write a book. He was never without work, and the lack of stress in his life made him content. If he had a wish, it would be that life would never change but that wish was short-lived.

Chapter 3

A ROUTINE LIFE

Jeremy was consistent with his routines — up at 7:00 a.m. each workday beginning his mornings with his typical coffee and cereal. He was dressed and ready for work by 8:30, but on the weekend he treated himself to an extra half hour of sleep. His weekend favorites were blueberry pancakes for breakfast and a brisk morning hike. Madison offered him many options for lone wilderness hikes with Rex by his side. His friend David, somewhat obese, was not into hiking or anything physical. David, reclusive and still living at home with his mom, spent hours gaming in front of his extra-large screen, captivated by the auditory and visual chaos. He was fortunate to have a mother who did not bug him too often to find a job or move out. She was accepting of his lifestyle in a distorted way rather than live alone. Both were stuck in the confines of a dysfunctional relationship seemingly without a way to resolve itself toward something better.

Since David was a confirmed bachelor like Jeremy, they enjoyed each other's uncomplicated and intellectually stimulating company. Almost every Saturday night they went to their favorite bar for their usual greasy food and beers. David was critical of the better looking dudes who lived a life that he secretly longed for. David saw himself as intellectually superior to them. His criticisms included penis size deficiency, if not outright impotence, bad haircut, bad breath, and all manner of unflattering acidic comments designed to make him and Jeremy look good. Though Jeremy didn't really share in David's condescending behavior, he indulged his friend until he found a way to change the subject. They both loved to talk about outer space, sci-fi, technologically weird and amazing advances, and the fate of the planet underscored with a spattering of conspiracy theories.

They both avoided discussions about religion or spirituality since David was a confirmed atheist. There were taboo subjects such as girls, sports, and family, choosing more comfortable conversations designed to stroke their egos. They were just two guys in a bar shooting the shit together — something repeated throughout the world in all its iterations. Once they had their fill of each other, they would head off home and resume their routines which varied little week by week. To others, this may have seemed a sad life filled with meaningless gestures. Both David and Jeremy gained great comfort in the steadiness and predictability of its rhythms; but this was about to change!

This Sunday's hike included a steep 3,000 foot climb up Mt. Edison. Jeremy and Rex climbed it easily, often scaling its heights, to the base of the pinnacle in a matter of a few hours. Its famous volcanic protrusion, remnants of an extinct volcano, was almost impossible to climb without the right gear. Jeremy was no mountaineer, merely a day hiker with little ambition to risk his life climbing the peak of the mountain. He was simply happy to get that far and enjoy the beautiful day.

Jeremy's goal was to reach the needle and eat his lunch there. September was his favorite month for outdoor activities, typically with clear skies, cooler temperatures, and beautiful fall colors. Rex was delirious with joy each time he and his master set out on a new adventure. Off-leash and free, he could explore all the smells, sights, and sounds, both master and hound relishing in this magical place.

They were both in tip-top shape, so the climb was easy enough. Oddly though, there was no one on the trail with them. The parking lot at the trailhead was empty except for Jeremy's vehicle. It seemed that they had the mountain to themselves, another bonus on this excellent day.

Jeremy loved the fresh air, the smells of fall, and the hint of winter to come. Rex busied himself chasing squirrels and hunting down the intriguing smells left behind by bigger creatures. As they climbed, their path crisscrossed the mountain; each switchback brought them closer to their intended goal. A slight breeze cooled them on their ascent and the trees shaded them from the heat of the sun. They soon reached their goal just in time for lunch. Jeremy selected a spot to sit among the boulders at the base of the needle, admiring the majesty of the place and glimpsing a view of the town below. Jeremy brought out a collapsible bowl, filling it with water for Rex. He was thankful for his master's care and attention and lapped it up until it was all gone.

Jeremy fancied himself as a bit of a cook, able to put flavors together in such a way that created a harmonious blend sure to please his palate. Today's lunch was no exception. He had grilled a steak with bell peppers the night before, and enlisted the leftovers to make him a steak and pepper sandwich on fresh bread from the local bakery. A nice wedge of cheese with a can of ice-cold beer was the perfect complement for his afternoon lunch.

The day was so pleasant that he decided after exploring around the needle's base to settle onto a spot of moss big enough to afford him a comfortable resting place. With birds chirping and Rex crouching down beside him, he soon fell into a deep sleep.

Chapter 4

AWAKENING TO DESTINY

Deep in sleep, Jeremy was aroused by a vision of a beautiful redhead caressing his cheek and quietly leaning in for a kiss. But he was rudely awakened from his vivid and pleasing dream by Rex barking madly at something close by. Swearing under his breath at the bad timing of his companion, he forced his eyes open and tried to orient himself to his surroundings. Rex, with his ruff up and stance in fight or flight mode, was focused on a man standing not more than a few feet away.

Once his awareness aligned with what his eyes were seeing, he too felt a rush of adrenaline and immediately got to his feet, stumbling in the process. Now upright, he focused on what was a very unnerving sight. The stranger gave the barking dog a serious look, causing Rex to stop and crouch down, shaking and furiously licking his muzzle in confusion. The man or at least he assumed it was a man, was tall, very tall, certainly over seven feet in height. He wore a long, faded blue robe that covered his feet. His face was not like any face he had seen before. It was long and narrow. He possessed high cheekbones and large oval eyes that were gold in color. They exuded warmth that was both compelling and disturbing. The man had an ample mouth framed by full lips, and his complexion was light blue with a hint of purple, highlighting a face that had an almost feminine look about it. His most inhuman feature was his nose, as it lacked normal definition. It looked as if a razor had cut through the nostrils, leaving behind a slight ridge over the nostrils, looking like two gashes that allowed him to breathe. He had a thin mantle of grey/green hair which hung almost to his shoulders. The image of Voldemort in the Harry Potter movies came to mind, except this creature seemed to have no ill intent as his face contorted into a human-like expression of concern as Jeremy reacted adversely to what he was seeing.

In Jeremy's mind, he heard a voice as clear and distinct as if it were his own say, 'Don't be afraid, I mean no harm and I come in peace'. Jeremy's first reaction was that he must be a character in his own sci-fi movie where the friendly alien said the same clichéd words to the wary humans upon first encounter. But he was not dreaming. Though the man before him seemed otherworldly and impossibly odd in appearance, he knew that he was awake and cognizant of what was happening. He swooned a bit with the full impact of his situation, feeling confused and disoriented. He was on the edge of fainting, but Jeremy was determined to stay present and alert to the apparent danger.

"You mean that you have been spying on me from your ship and abducting me at night while I've been asleep so that you can experiment on me?" Jeremy responded in a fearsome if not wavering voice. The man laughed out loud, this time audibly through his prominent mouth. Jeremy was nonplussed by this response. He was sure that he had been the victim of serious abuse and though shaking with fear, he was determined to get to the bottom of this bizarre encounter.

"I have great love and respect for you Jeremy and would never think of violating your person in any way," said the man telepathically. "Where I come from, such things are unheard of and certainly never expressed. We are a peaceable people, seeking light and harmony. We wish to serve the universe in love, assisting our soulful cousins in universal progression toward truth and the fulfillment of their personal journey in light. I have come to help you to realize this in your own life Jeremy. We are what you humans will become one day, and we are here to help you realize your potential and expression of it."

Jeremy didn't know what to make of this so-called friend and wondered how he knew his name? He didn't seem to fit into his assumptions about aliens, angels or demons. He had read plenty on these subjects but to encounter someone like this firsthand was nothing like he imagined. His suspicions were not allayed by the man's eloquent talk of friendship nor his offer to assist Jeremy in such an esoteric way. After all, Jeremy was a simple man, not seeking tutoring on universal truths and the fundamentals of the cosmos. All he desired at the moment was for everything to return to normal, and that this man would vanish into thin air so that he and Rex could head for home while passing off this encounter as an anomaly of his overactive imagination.

Picking up on Jeremy's desire to break off the encounter, the man bid him farewell for now and before they were to part, he said "You can call me Orion and we will meet again, this I promise you." And as if Orion heard his unspoken desires, he vanished.

Jeremy descended down the mountain in record time, running as fast as he could, putting as much distance between him and the 'creature' with every step. Rex too felt the urgency of the situation and barked incessantly as they ran. The vision of Orion was still fresh in his mind, and no matter how fast he ran it dominated his vision. The entire encounter played over and over again until he finally reached his car. He and Rex piled in, feeling safer now as they screeched home.

Some relief came with their return to familiar territory, yet all the while, Jeremy was vigilant and worried that he was destined to be abducted in his sleep or at any moment. There was no rest for Jeremy that night. Rex remained on guard as they stayed close throughout the night. Nothing seemed the same and everything had a sense of malevolence and unfamiliarity as Jeremy tried to calm himself, each hour ticking by without much comfort or ease from his fear. He was a changed man and just how changed would be something completely unanticipated.

Chapter 5

A Friend Indeed

Although several weeks had passed, Jeremy could not shake off his troubling encounter. It was a constant reminder every time he looked toward the mountain, whether he was in town or even from his back porch. He began to curse the day that he hiked up there, ruining what was once an often-treasured time of replenishment and solitude. His dreams were haunted by Orion's presence, stealing Jeremy's hope for a peaceful, deep sleep. They were not nightmares, but dim whispers from Orion, "We will meet again." It caused Jeremy to wake with a start, drenched in sweat.

He told his friend David about his encounter during their usual Saturday night outings. David was undecided about Jeremy's story. On one hand, he knew Jeremy to be a straight shooter, never prone to exaggeration or hysteria, but on the other hand, this story seemed completely fabricated. He thought of Moses on the Mount encountering the burning bush and the voice of God. He knew that Jeremy had his spiritual beliefs, but he didn't know the extent of them. Either Jeremy was losing it or his buddy was on to something. He smiled and encouraged him to keep his antennas open and see what more this guy wanted to tell him. Jeremy took little comfort in his friend's words, yet something deep inside him knew that indeed there was going to be more from Orion in the future. In truth, David thought but did not say that the whole thing would blow over in a few weeks. He chalked it up to some delusional thinking. Maybe he accidentally ate a weird mushroom, or had a freak psychotic break that brought on the experience. Whatever it was, David hoped that he had heard enough of this weirdness.

Jeremy had been restless and unhappy for weeks — often cranky and impatient with his customers. It was similar to having PTSD and showed as he tried to resume his life after the incident.

At his weekly Tuesday visit with Muriel, she was keenly aware of Jeremy's distress. He was off his game and she was compelled to find out why. So, she tentatively asked him in her gentle, yet refined, English accent, "How are you doing Jeremy? You seem a bit preoccupied, and I'm worried about you." He could not help but melt into soft sobs of pain and anguish. Her sweet grandmotherly approach opened the floodgates of Jeremy's heart and the story of his bizarre encounter gushed forth with all its disturbing details.

This didn't faze Muriel. She had lived long enough to know that the depth and breadth of human experience encompassed all manner of weird and extraordinary things. Though Jeremy's story seemed highly unusual and probably unlikely, she stayed with him, composed and listening intently as the story unfolded to its conclusion. "Well," she said in an exaggerated look of bewilderment, "I have never heard such an interesting story." She was thinking that poor Jeremy had fallen off the deep end, and that all those years of living alone with no lady friend to keep him on the straight and narrow had taken its toll. "No wonder you have been feeling so discombobulated lately," she said with true motherly concern. "Your mind has been taken for a ride that you couldn't possibly have anticipated, and you are trying to cope with this horrible encounter by yourself," she said as gently as she could.

"You need help. Don't get me wrong. I don't mean a psychiatrist, I mean someone like Sadie Jenkins, who wouldn't blink an eye at such an unusual story." Muriel said with the utmost of confidence.

"You mean that weird lady who lives out on Miller's Corner?" he said with a bit of disdain.

"Yes, she's someone who I believe can help" Muriel said while nodding her head in affirmation. "Whenever I have had a pressing problem in my life, I always go to her for one of her readings. She straightens me out every time and I think that she can do the same for you son."

Of course, Jeremy was skeptical, but he was also aware that people like Sadie Jenkins can see things others can't. After all, in his youth and childhood, he also had the gift of sight. Having had unseen friends in childhood, he later closed down this propensity in favor of a more orthodox perspective of the world. He also knew things before they would happen, and he could sense what people were really like. Even with his now diminished intuition, it was enough to keep him distant from a lot of people. He would rather have his present close-knit circle of friends and associates than venture out into the wider world. But now his world had become shattered, topsy-turvy, no up or down, just the chaos of mental disorientation and anxiety. Maybe he was going crazy, and even dear sweet Muriel could sense this wicked turn of events in him. He shouldn't have broken down in tears — what a stupid thing to do, he thought to himself. To cry like a baby in front of Mrs. Phelps was not only unprofessional but also left the door open for her to disapprove of him. He certainly didn't want to lose her as a friend and customer. He had been through enough and was not up for more problems in his life.

His demeanor changed abruptly. In a formal voice designed to indicate a regained sense of composure, he said, "Thank you Mrs. Phelps, I'll certainly consider your advice. I'm deeply sorry if I have upset you and I'll get back to work now. Thanks for the tea and cake." At that, he got out of his chair to go back to work.

Muriel was not at all convinced that Jeremy would follow up with Sadie, but she was determined to keep the suggestion alive in his mind. "Oh, not a problem, dear," she said with motherly compassion. "Please take my idea seriously; I just know that she can help."

Both Muriel and Jeremy got back to their respective chores without any further word spoken about this lapse of decorum. Their bond of friendship was deep and respectful, but Jeremy disliked being vulnerable in this way and felt that he had crossed a line with her. He was determined to never do that again. He wanted his reputation to be intact and hoped that Mrs. Phelps would keep quiet about this unprofessional encounter.

The day ended as it always did, with Muriel praising his work, adding a little tip to his bill, and a promise that they would see each other next week. They fit so well together, always engaging in stimulating conversation and providing much-needed mutual support. This form of love was hard to come by in this world and they both knew that there was something special about their bond. Yet, Jeremy's situation had caused a ripple in an otherwise glassy pond, and he hoped that all would be forgotten in good time. How wrong he was.

Chapter 6

THE TRUTH UNADORNED

Although several weeks had passed, Jeremy's mental state and sleep habits had not improved. Whenever he saw Muriel Phelps, she would ask if he had been to see Sadie Jenkins. The answer was always the same. "No Mrs. Phelps, I'm doing ok and I don't think that I need her help now."

Muriel sensed otherwise and kept up her campaign to get him to go at least once. This polite battle of wills went on for several more weeks, and Muriel even offered to pay for the session! Over time, Jeremy's resolve weakened and he finally agreed to go. How could he say no to her generosity and sincerity? He wanted to appease Muriel's hopes for him, but dreaded meeting with whom the town considered the local w¬itch.

Although Sadie Jenkins was an eccentric, she did not seem to be that crazy or strange. Rather, she tended a beautiful garden that surrounded her ramshackle cottage deeply in need of some TLC. It was obvious that Sadie was not rich. She maintained a modest lifestyle by selling herbs and performing healings for folks in need of interventions beyond the capacity of local doctors. Although these efforts provided her with some income, the bulk of it came from Tarot card readings, where she excelled with accuracy.

Sadie was in her sixties, a little worn around the edges. She was the daughter of a Virginian coal miner and had moved west to get away from her family and the oppressive atmosphere of her hometown. She had that rounded mother earth appearance that conveyed an aging body but a vital spirit. Sadie dressed like an old hippie with long caftans supplemented by an old, tattered brown shawl. Her dark brown hair was often covered by a scarf, similar to Aunt Jemima on the pancake box. Her face was plump and a bit florid, belying her ancestry from the *old country*. Her eyes were her most striking feature, a deep blue with a hint of hazel, and they missed nothing! She had a look about her that meant business and few would argue with her to her face. The folks who made that mistake would discover the hardscrabble Sadie who never backed down from a fight. Her smile, however, could melt the heart of anyone who was in her presence. She was an interesting amalgam of hard and soft. The hard covering up a very soft side she guarded well.

She came from a long line of psychics and seers on her mother's side. Such things were not uncommon where she lived as a child, but she rarely talked about. Her mother's gift became obvious when she would set the table for an unexpected guest who showed up at the last minute unannounced. She and other gifted seers often predicted unexpected deaths in the family. To the chagrin of her father and others who were not gifted in the same way, they doggedly accepted that these women could see things that they could not.

Sadie knew her spirit guides and helpers well. Almost daily she would meet many diverse souls in need of support and guidance. What greater blessing than to serve her fellow man in ways that others could not? She had a deep faith in God, not the kind that people proclaimed at church, but a simple daily practice that brought her to the Source in quiet prayer. Simply knowing that she was loved, and receiving the Creator's divine love in daily prayer brought her great peace and insight. It nurtured her soul like nothing else could. Her gifts developed from childhood flooding her with true spiritual light. She did not speak openly about her gifts for fear of scaring people away. She knew the angels were with her, providing answers to not only her questions and dilemmas, but to others as well. Humble yet firm, she helped a lot of people who were lost and overwhelmed. They felt at peace when Sadie spoke to them and, her home-spun wisdom offered guidance to many.

Muriel Phelps's hunch that Sadie could help poor Jeremy sort out his problems was confirmed by Jeremy's visit to Sadie's house. Jeremy was wary as he approached the door. Knocking hesitantly, he prepared himself to be confronted by the *old witch*. But gazing into her garden reassured him and eased his fears. He could see that the rhythms and beauty of her garden were not created by happenstance, but by true knowledge and creativity.

As he knocked, he heard an abrupt *come in* from the other side of the door. When he opened the door and noticed Sadie's demeanor, he became nervous. She seemed a bit rude and stern at first. Her house smelled of mold and cat urine. She had a lot of cats, seemingly dozens. The tiny home was cluttered with drying herbs, dust, knick-knacks, tattered furniture, and cats reclining everywhere.

"Close the door quickly," she told him with a somewhat terse retort. "I don't want any cats running out into the street. I lost one the other day from a crazed teen screeching through the neighborhood in his hopped-up jalopy. That kid is a tragedy in the making' she said in a plaintive voice." "I've talked to his parents — my neighbors, but they won't listen, and I can't waste my time talking to a pair of brick walls."

"Enough said on that subject," said Sadie abruptly, as she lifted a cat off the chair opposite her and gestured for Jeremy to have a seat in front of her. "We have more important things to discuss than the state of the neighborhood."

"So, what brings you here?" while giving him a knowing look. "Or more to the point, are you ready to talk now, boy, since I know that you are keeping a big secret inside of you that needs prying out?"

An awkward silence befell the room as Jeremy considered her blunt question and how best to answer her in a way that didn't make him sound like a lunatic. Sadie's piercing eyes offered him no opportunity to gain a semblance of composure. As a cat jumped up onto his lap, purring loudly, he began to stutter out his abridged version of the event. He recited the details of the experience that had been weighing on him so heavily. His words were slow and deliberate. It portrayed a sense of deep caution as he spoke. All through his recitation, Sadie gave knowing nods as her eyes brightened with recognition.

She already knew Jeremy's story. She had been dreaming the same story for some months now and it had been a relief to finally hear it in person. When she saw Jeremy enter her home, she instantly knew that they were to become partners in a very intriguing adventure, one that would lead to extraordinary events in both their lives.

When Jeremy finished, Sadie in her most gentle voice said, "You are not going crazy Jeremy. You had an extraordinary experience that can be a great gift to you if you are willing to accept it" she said with quiet confidence.

"Although you might think that this experience was some sort of fluke or a one-off event. It was neither, and your friend who calls himself Orion had planned this meeting all along," Sadie assured him while reaching out and gently touching his knee.

Jeremy's eyes widened as he knew that he purposely didn't tell her the name of his visitor for fear of invoking his presence. "How did you know his name?" he asked in astonishment. "Are you one of them?" he blurted out before his mind could censor his thoughts.

Sadie was amused and tried to stifle a smile. "No Jeremy, I'm not one of them, merely human like you, from Terra Firma. But I am acquainted with Orion as we have had the odd conversation together. I like him very much and I consider him a friend," she said quietly.

"He is your friend too Jeremy. That I know for certain, as I have been aware of you for quite some time, waiting for you to come and see me so that we could have this conversation," she said without hesitation.

Jeremy was at the point of fleeing from this *witch*. How could she know so much and how could she say that she is a friend of this creature? The tension in his body indicated that he was preparing to flee. At that very moment, Orion appeared in front of Sadie and told her to be silent and pray. He said that he would calm the boy and help him to understand the situation.

Jeremy instantly felt a wave of peace come over him — a quality of peace that he had never felt before. His body was heavy with it and a light sense of drowsiness overcame him. The atmosphere was thick with something so different and appealing that he slumped into his chair and had no further impulse to go. He wondered what the witch was doing to him. "Some sort of spell, I suppose, "he said under his breath. But he could not move, and resigned himself to enjoying this pleasurable state of being.

Sadie began to straighten in her chair, displaying a puckered expression on her face. Then she began to speak. Not in her usual lyrical way but in what can only be described as a man's voice, deep and resonant. "My friend," she said clearly and distinctly. "I told you a while back that we would meet again and here I am at your service, it is Orion."

Still, some part of Jeremy's mind was trying to muster up enough momentum to get out of his chair and flee. He couldn't do it, because a greater part of him was happy to remain. Damn *witch* he thought.

Orion went on to say that he had a plan that involved the three of them in a venture to educate the world of the true nature of life as it relates to the fabric of the universe. His intentions were to help humanity see the folly of their ways as the Earth becomes further degraded by human endeavors which are contrary to basic universal laws. He continued to explain that humanity was on the verge of either self-annihilation or opening up the door to truly discovering themselves. He went on to speculate that it will probably be both at once. He told Jeremy that he was to become an integral part of such a plan; and that through the gifts of my dear friend here, he would begin to help Jeremy understand sophisticated knowledge about what is, and how to go about finding truth. That Jeremy had a wealth of untapped gifts which could be used to awaken others to this truth.

"It will involve a substantial commitment of time from you my friend, as these things are not readily understood nor are they easy to impart. But I see in you the possibility of being a willing and open student to what I have to teach and assist you in the task of discovering what is truly you Jeremy Flynn. We have the opportunity to embark on a journey the likes of which you could not possibly imagine. The question is as you might expect. Are you willing to join us in this venture? This can be a turning point in your life so crucial and powerful that you will not look back, rather, to continue to move forward as a beautiful conduit of light and truth. You have a destiny my boy, which is most unusual and highly unconventional. Yet, since you are meant to follow this road, it is unlikely that you would be happy diverting yourself from it."

"The choice always remains with you, Jeremy. Are you willing to take up the challenge presented to you?" asked Orion in a very serious tone. "Consider this invitation with all your heart and mind as it is the most important decision you will ever make."

He sensed Orion was leaving, but as he went, he gave Jeremy a vision of his home planet. A place rich with life but the color pallet was all wrong. The color of the sky was primarily magenta with clouds purple and pink. The glade he was standing in was not so much green but dappled with shades of blue and shadows of vermillion with deep crimson. Some green existed there but was by no means the most predominant color present. The stream he stood beside sparkled with flecks of gold and diamond flashes that reflected the light so intensely that he was mesmerized by its patterns dancing in his vision as the water flowed. Jeremy thought of an acid trip that he had taken long ago and how his reality morphed into fantastic shapes and colors just like what was happening to him presently.

The air smelled fresh and fragrant with nearby blossoms — fragrances that he had never known before. The sun shone, but upon closer inspection, it was not just one sun but two. One shone more brightly while its companion seemed to wash out the shadows and further illuminate the scene before him. It was the most exotic and beautiful scene that he had ever encountered. Like being immersed in a magical photograph, altered in such a way to make it look surreal. Everything was alive and in motion. It was not a dream at all, but rather an experience more vivid than life itself.

Instantly he was back in Sadie's small living room, taking in its own very real sights and smells, yet still somewhat immersed in his surreal daydream. He had a look of serenity on his face, complemented by a big grin. If he was under the influence of some hallucinogenic drug, then it was the best trip he had ever had. The truth was much stranger than that, however. Orion had shown him something extraordinary, something he would never forget. All thoughts of Sophie being some kind of a witch and Orion an evil alien were replaced by a sense of peace and that all was well in the world.

Sadie too had a look of great serenity on her face. Her eyes were closed with head tilted back as if dozing in her chair. Her favorite cat, George was purring and kneading on her shoulder, waking her from her reverie. They both looked at each other, instantly recognizing that they had the same experience —armchair travelers to a different world.

Chapter 7

TAKING STOCK

It took a while for Jeremy and Sadie to compose themselves after such an intense experience. Jeremy's fears and apprehensions evaporated as he came back from this unexpected journey to Orion's planet. He and Sadie were now bonded through this shared experience. They returned refreshed and at peace despite it being so bizarre. They both knew that they had not been taken up in a spacecraft. It was not like that at all. Instead, it was a shift of consciousness and location that was instantaneous, like a flip of a switch that took them beyond their limitations of consciousness. Although an hour had gone by, they both sensed that their experience was without any time constraints. They each mused quietly in thought, searching for explanations about their very strange, but fascinating experience, unable to articulate what had just happened. So they sat together without words for a while.

There was little doubt that it was real, but they had trouble reconciling the event with real-world parameters. Sadie, of course, had more experience with such things but had never known something quite so exotic and tangible. It surprised her almost as much as it surprised Jeremy

She was unsure about how to restart their conversation after such an unusual event. Since she was the more experienced psychic traveler, she began. "Well Jeremy, do you believe me now? Orion wants us to go on this journey together," quickly reverting back to her usual gruff voice.

"I, I don't know what to think," Jeremy replied with a stutter. He had to acknowledge that what had taken place was both weird and wonderful at the same time. This did not help him in his resolve to let the whole matter go. Instead, he was gob smacked with a sense of wonder and inner joy — the complete opposite of his intention to distance himself from Orion, and Sadie! Similar to his first Orion encounter, it all seemed implausible and yet, it had to be real! As the reverie of the moment began to fade, the question in his mind was how to reconcile these things with his present life. An inner war of wills raged within his head, as he tried to fuse together the normalcy of his material life with all of the things that have happened outside of it.

It all seemed too much and he asked Sadie in an almost pleading manner, "How do you cope with stuff like this? Although I wouldn't call you a woman who follows all the rules, you do seem ok and not completely crazy!"

Sadie gave a sardonic smile. "I've been called worse my friend. It hasn't been an easy life and yes, I could have denied my gifts with all its challenges. But I chose differently and dear boy, at this juncture, you too will have to make this choice. Are you in or are you out?" she asked without any hint of persuasion. "We can't do this alone. We need each other since Orion brought us together for a reason."

There was some comfort in knowing that he had a friend on this unprecedented journey, even though his mind was full of doubts and suspicions about Sadie. What were her motives and were they honorable? Was this just a game so that Sadie could suck him into her elaborate plot to seduce him and indenture him into serving her material and maybe sexual needs?"

Sadie sensed his resistance and lack of trust. "Jeremy, you don't need to decide at this very moment but the sooner you resolve your inner dilemmas, the sooner we can get to work." Sadie got up and opened the door adding, "It is my sincere hope, Jeremy, that you will come back and very soon," while giving him a piercing look. "For now, I have other things to attend to as I have no doubt you do as well."

Jeremy left, bewildered, content, and discombobulated at the same time. On the drive home, his mind was swimming in a sea of conjecture while trying to piece together his thoughts into some semblance of order about what had happened and how far this would go. He had the comfort of Rex resting his head on Jeremy's knee and the further he got from Sadie's house, the more doubt flooded in.

Chapter 8

THE CHOICE

After a good night's sleep, Jeremy woke up with a sense that something very strange was happening to him. Yet, whatever it was, it felt good! It was like falling in love, but not with a woman, but with life itself. After his otherworldly experience at Sadie's house, there had been a big shift in attitude and perception deep inside him. His usual cautious and often guarded approach to life was replaced by effusive optimism, and a never-before sense that all is going to be well. He was happy, and those often-felt threads of anxiety that bound him to a constricted life were simply not there anymore. Whatever Orion and his sidekick Sadie had done to him, he was grateful. But he still held some suspicions about why he was the subject of such a weird and extraordinary series of events. It was very clear that something fundamental had changed and he deeply wished it would continue on forever.

Muriel Phelps had also noticed a big difference in Jeremy's demeanor. He was cheerful, had a buoyant lift in his step and a constant grin on his face. Whatever Sadie had helped him with, it had done the trick and Muriel was pleased as punch.

She approached the subject somewhat cautiously. She didn't want him to feel intruded upon, remembering the last time they had a personal conversation and how he responded with embarrassment, quickly shutting down. "Well, you seem to be a happy man this morning," quipped Muriel in her usual lyrical way. "Do you have anything different to report dear boy?" she asked, with a quizzical but gentle tone. Jeremy took the bait immediately.

"Nothing has really changed, Mrs. Phelps, but in a way, everything has changed. You were right about Sadie, she has quite a way about her," he said, apologetically. "I wish that I had seen her sooner, she answered a lot of questions about the incident. I think that I am going to go back. I want to get deeper into it," he said without hesitation.

"Oh, I am so very pleased for you Jeremy. Yes, Sadie is quite an interesting person, isn't she? She can be a bit overbearing at times, but she has a heart of gold, and you can trust her with your secrets and vulnerabilities. I have never known her to betray a confidence," she added with a knowing smile.

"I certainly hope that I can trust her, Mrs. Phelps, because what she is proposing we do together is a bit out there," said Jeremy in his usual understated way. He didn't mention Orion's communication to him because he thought that revealing this part of his visit was too strange and unbelievable even for Mrs. Phelps.

"I don't believe you will be disappointed in her Jeremy," Muriel smiled with assurance. "I've known her for over 40 years, and we have become quite good friends. Yes, she is a bit eccentric like so many people with a creative approach to life." I consider you a part of my creative circle, Jeremy, and I think that you are going places that others have not been." She excused herself and went into the house — as always, well-timed and polite.

Jeremy thought about what Muriel had said about Sadie and about himself. Her words felt reassuring, and offered a familiar kindness that he knew well with Muriel. She had been a consistent and reliable friend for many years. He knew she possessed a depth of wisdom that no one else had. Her words rang true — not in a mindful way, but in a way that resounded deep in his heart. He now knew the answer he would give to both Sadie and Orion. He was in, despite the trepidation his mind felt as he made his resolve. His life until now seemed bland and safe. Never had he embarked on such an unusual venture, yet deep inside he felt relief and joy. He was going to contradict all his well-worn rules of engagement and team up with the local witch and her otherworldly friend. He knew that on this chosen road, there would be no turning back and nothing predictable —an adventure of a lifetime.

Chapter 9

THE COMMITMENT

As the days passed after Jeremy's first visit with Sadie, he became more consumed with questions. He felt his only solution was to book another appointment with her. He was concerned with the time and costs it would require of him. Not only were his funds limited, but his time away from work and responsibilities were limited as well. Would he seriously commit his time and valued resources to this bizarre, but exciting venture? He was determined to approach these questions with as much diplomacy as he could muster before affirming his desire to join Sadie in this venture.

Sadie, with her usual curt greeting, bade him to enter and sit down. She wanted to finish reading a letter from a heartsick client in need of counseling. As usual, the scent of drying herbs unsuccessfully masked less inviting smells. In time he would get used to this challenging environment. In fact, he would grow to appreciate it in such a way that it felt like home. For now, however, it was a foreign land that confronted Jeremy's conventional views of how one should live. Sadie was an enigma and a curiosity that he had trouble reconciling in his mind. If it were not for deeper feelings of wonder and excitement, he would have decided to stay away for good. Mrs. Phelps helped him to see a deeper side of this unusual woman, and he reassured himself that he was headed in the right direction.

Sadie finished reading her letter and removed her reading glasses, allowing them to drop onto her ample bosom. The glasses gave her round face a sense of studiousness and highlighted her high cheekbones. She was a plump, but not grossly large woman. Short in height, her somewhat hunched frame belied her 60-plus years on this earth. Although still sturdy and tough enough to deal with the physical requirements of her present life, she suffered with serious defects in her heart, along with chronic high blood pressure. Even though she looked well, she in fact was not as well as she appeared. She often wore bright colored caftans or Mumus so that she was comfortable while performing her work. Her long hair was tied up into a loose bun secured by a single chopstick.

Jeremy felt nervous with anticipation. Sadie sensed his excitement and his ambivalence. "Welcome back Jeremy," Sadie began. "I'm sure that you have some news for me today," she said with a twinkle in her eyes, anticipating his inquiries.

"Well, I have a few questions that I hope you may answer," Jeremy said in his usual slow-paced speech. "I'm not a rich man," he continued. "I have to work for a living at a job that pays enough for my needs, but I don't have much left over. I don't want to be rude; but I am concerned about the costs of your services."

Sadie was inwardly amused, but she played the game with a straight face. "Are you afraid that this dime store psychic will shackle you with debt, or are you enthralled and helpless to resist my wishes? Are you truly concerned about money at this stage of the game dear boy?" she said with a sly smile on her face. Oh, she was enjoying watching him squirm through this difficult but ridiculous conversation.

"I need to ask these questions dear lady because, if I am to commit to such an unusual task, I need to know what I'm dealing with," he said as he squirmed.

"Yes, indeed, you do dear boy, but are you asking the right questions? What about the adventure that has been offered to you by our friend from a different world? What about the need to prepare yourself for such an adventure?" Quietly spoken with the conviction of a sage and saleswoman, she asked," Do you think that you are ready to put caution to the wind and climb abroad this trip of a lifetime?"

"Jeremy, I have no intention of charging you for my services, as you most delicately put it," she said with amusement. I wouldn't dream of it because in this arrangement, we are to be equal partners along with Orion. There will be no service charge per se, just two souls embarking on a very intriguing journey. It is an enterprise that neither of us truly understands. We were chosen, Jeremy, for reasons neither you nor I can explain. But here we are two peas in a pod, hopefully, able to play our part with aplomb and with eyes wide open."

Sadie's eloquent response took Jeremy back a bit. He was expecting to dicker with her using his somewhat rudimentary business skills gained from a life of self-employment. A deal needed to be made, and he was determined to make one that benefited both. Instead, she gave him the keys without any fight at all and it took him a few moments to respond. When he regained his composure, he blurted out "I can help you with your house and your garden too." He had offered her everything he could give without truly considering the consequences. "It's obvious that you need some help around here and I can be your man around this place."

Sadie was secretly delighted by his offer as it was indeed obvious that she could use the help, but she didn't want him to feel obligated and indentured to her needs — rather, to be in harmony with mutual support. She hoped that what he might give in a material sense, she could reciprocate spiritually. In harmony of universal balance, there would be some understanding that what was given would be rewarded in whatever way the Creator would provide.

She knew that there was a plan, something important, even profound, and that when the right souls are brought together in this way, wonderful outcomes could be expected. She could see Jeremy's inner light — his simple integrity and approach to life. He just needed a boost to a higher level of consciousness, something that she could do for him. In truth, she had not been so excited about spiritual work like this for a very long time. She knew that there was a gift coming into her life that was important and transformative, but she didn't know when and what form it would take. Yet, before her was the beginning of it in the form of this humble and simple man who had no idea of his destiny journey and the gifts he carried. For now, she needed to be composed and not overly effusive. She needed to reassure him that she could be trusted and that she was honorable. She had to tread softly at this critical juncture and offer him explanations that he could accept, given the circumstances.

"Jeremy," she said clearly and with compassion, "you have a significant and very unique destiny. I have never met anyone who is so full of potential. I see it in your auric field, multiple colors dancing and weaving together. Most have a mixture of light and dark, indicating a variety of conflicts and gifts within them. But you are filled with light and promise. Today marks the beginning of a new life for you Jeremy — a life filled with extraordinary experiences, growth, and transformation. As time goes by, you will understand what I am saying but for now, I need you to merely trust in the process. I would counsel you to contemplate, even pray about what it is you really want out of life. You can't truly move forward without being clear about your desires and goals. Your mind needs focusing, and your heart needs to be in the right place. This will be a full-on journey that will be in part an intellectual awakening, but most importantly, something far deeper within you will stir and open the way to many gifts that for now you don't understand. It will be a soul-changing experience, and it will be something unlike anything you have experienced. You need to be prepared and grounded."

"I believe that this should be enough conversation for one day," advised Sadie. "We'll start off slow and since you have had little experience in trans-mediumship communication, I'll give you a book to guide you." She handed him a thin book entitled Trans-Mediumship for the Beginner, authored by Harold F. Courtney, published in 1953. Jeremy again a little bewildered and with a loss for words, accepted Sadie's book and left without a goodbye.

Sadie knew that Jeremy couldn't resist what was being offered even if he had his doubts. Yet, now was a time of tying up loose ends and starting with a fresh outlook and clarity. She left it to the Creator and Orion to help Jeremy find his way into this new life and way of looking at the world.

Chapter 10

TUESDAYS

The book that Sadie gave Jeremy helped him to understand her unusual gifts and abilities to communicate with spirits not part of this world. He felt as if he had gained a new lease on life. A complete reversal as his dark dreams and anxiety morphed into visions of bizarre but beautiful revelations. Things still not understood filled him with wonder. Although Orion had appeared as a corporal body, he made contact using his spirit body aptly described in the book that Sadie lent him. It described a gift we all possess, having a body that persists in all of us after death. Jeremy had heard of spiritualism before but perceived it as a delusional concept. His reading helped him make sense of their communication with Orion — no spaceships or abductions were required. Orion was there with them in thought and intention, using his spirit body and consciousness as the only vehicle necessary for communication.

He began to realize that the vast majority of people in the world had no concept of the spirit world, nor did they realize that life in this world was only a precursor to a greater life that existed, referred to as the spirit spheres. He learned that everyone had to progress beyond their present spiritual condition in order to enter into successive higher levels of spirit existence which were filled with light and joy. Amazingly, even the most wretched individual had the potential to reach new worlds of beauty and joy in these spheres. They only needed the desire to right the wrongs of earthly life and adopt new, more loving ways of being. These new revelations filled Jeremy with an openness and optimism and he sensed that it was right and true. What he once considered highly improbable now made perfect sense and is likely true.

Jeremy and Sadie began to settle into a routine together every Tuesday. After the morning session and lunch, Jeremy would spend a few hours repairing her home or tending her garden. She prepared flavorful soups, home-baked bread, and some of their favorite desserts. Sadie had a list of ongoing chores — eaves to be repaired and cleaned, dry rot on the back porch, weeding, and much more. He was happy to put his skills to good use, giving him as much satisfaction as it did his newfound patron.

He quickly bonded to Sadie's world, something he never imagined when they first met. She soon felt like family, not only as a dear friend but more like a second mother. She was more loving and understanding than his own mother. The relationship with Sadie felt deeper and more resonant with his present needs. His mother's expectations of him were different than what he felt he could fulfill. Sadie's approach was more spiritual and less demanding of him. She praised him often and continued to explain many deeper aspects of his nature in a way that made sense to him, helping him feel both safe and seen. The timing of their relationship seemed right, as it continued to grow and unfold as their sense of purpose with one another gained greater depth.

This did not develop merely by chance. It was all orchestrated by their mutual friend Orion whose abilities to influence and guide were formidable. His plan was unfolding beautifully, and he was indeed pleased with how the relationship between the two was blooming

Jeremy had many questions about Sadie's mediumship and how she could talk to the dead. She explained that the dead are more alive than we are. The world of spirit allows many more possibilities of expression, especially creative expression. She went on to say that since we all possess a spirit body, which is not restricted by the needs and limitations of the physical body, the requirements to sustain life are far fewer in the spirit world. Spirits are able to move, communicate, and express themselves in ways that are not yet possible on this material plane. Individuality and personality are not lost either; instead each soul has a greater depth of knowing who they are, opening the door to more possibilities of development and expression of their own unique gifts. She affirmed her own readiness to transition into the spirit world. She quipped that she has had a full life on earth and is looking forward to the next step.

Sadie was sure that many people are capable of communication with the spirit realms, but few take it seriously enough to pursue it. As the daughter of a long line of psychic women, she had always been drawn to spiritual matters and studied many philosophies in her youth. At one point she thought that she would become a minister, but upon meeting a gifted psychic by the name of Peter Marshal, her ambitions took a very different direction. Peter immediately saw her potential as a medium, and offered to mentor her in the art of spirit communication. The relationship went well for a few years, but eventually the older man's unwelcome sexual advances put an end to it. She had learned enough from him to set her on a lifelong course of service and dedication collaborating with the spirits.

She told Jeremy that mediumship was not that complicated, one only needed to let go and allow a spirit to establish a rapport. She emphasized that it was important to connect with higher level spirits who had the best intentions. Discernment was necessary with the intention of the medium to obtain spiritual guidance and a blessing of light was the key to success. Although, it was easier to establish a connection with spirits on the lower plain who were at the beginning of their spiritual development.

After several more sessions and continued study of the book on trans-mediumship, Jeremy began to understand why he often sensed things that others didn't. He certainly didn't think of himself as gifted in the way that she was, but he saw similarities in thought and perception. He gained great comfort in the knowledge that someone understood him, and related to him in ways that no one else did. As an outlier in a very material world, he felt like he belonged in Sadie's world, though bizarre and unorthodox. He looked forward to every Tuesday so that they could continue with their spiritual truth conversations.

Indeed, Sadie was all too eager to engage with Jeremy. She had a sense that they belonged together –something that she had never experienced with another person. They were simpatico in their thoughts and perceptions, which completed the picture of one another. This unlikely pair found love and comfort in their friendship. Each expressed themselves with an ease that transcended all differences. It was clear that Sadie was the teacher but what teacher did not feel great satisfaction in guiding a willing student towards enlightenment? Thus, the bonding of Sadie and Jeremy was complete, setting the stage for continued collaboration with Orion.

Chapter 11

MOVING FORWARD

Jeremy and Sadie's in-depth conversations about the spirit world continued for several more weeks. During this time, Sadie was able to get to know and understand Jeremy better and eventually felt confident that he was ready to enter the next level. It was now time to add Orion into the mix. Giving him the opportunity to communicate his wishes to them both. Each had their role to play. Orion was obviously the teacher and Jeremy his student. However, without the mediumistic gifts that Sadie possessed, this could not be accomplished. She was the vital circuit in the process. Though Orion possessed a corporal body, it was far easier for him to travel to Earth using his spirit, or ethereal body, than to physically travel the vast distance between their two planets. Sadie's gifts allowed Orion to impress on her mind what he wished to say since it was not an easy task for him to manifest, as he originally did to Jeremy, every time he wished to communicate. Without her, the possibility of such detailed communication would be very unlikely and exceedingly difficult. Sadie taught Jeremy everything she knew about this form of communication, but he couldn't truly understand it beyond the fact that she was not conveying her own thoughts but those of somebody else. It was an act of faith on Jeremy's part to believe that it was real and trust was built on hours of conversation between them. And so, the time was ripe, and they entered their three-way communications.

One afternoon, after Jeremy had completed a home repair for Sadie, she suggested that they sit in prayer and meditation for a time in order to hear from Orion. She began, as she always did before opening herself to communication with spirits, with a heartfelt prayer.

"Beloved Creator of the universe," she began, "Bring us closer to the source of all love, your love, and help us to attune ourselves to it, receiving this essence into our souls evermore."

As she said these words, the atmosphere in the room changed palpably as a blanket of peace descended upon them, bringing with it an inexplicable sense that they were not alone.

She continued praying with the words "Take us beyond this place of flesh and pain to realms of light and truth. Allow us the gift of communing with those bright spirits and angels who wish to uphold us. Our desire is to communicate in clarity and truth with our stellar friend whom we call Orion. May your will be done, beloved Creator so that we may serve a higher purpose in accordance with your plan to uplift us all in the truth of love." With this she whispered amen and fell into what seemed like a deep sleep.

Jeremy felt a twinge of excitement mixed with reverence. It was another new experience, one of many, as he and Sadie grew in their friendship. He believed in God and prayed deeply during times of desperate need and comfort, but he had not felt as expansive and hopeful as he did now. It's as if a world had opened up that had always been at his fingertips, but unreachable merely because he didn't really know how to pray. Sadie showed him how, with her sincere and humble ways to invoke Divine blessings for them both and his sense of gratitude and awe grew every time they prayed.

A few moments passed and Sadie's rhythmic deep breathing shortened into something shallower. This concerned Jeremy, thinking she was in some distress. Nothing could be further from the truth as she continued to climb higher into an experience of reverie and longing for God. Within minutes, she lost consciousness altogether, signaling a different but familiar phase of physiology, both within her brain and body. She had entered into a trance state, facilitating communication with a spirit as her breathing changed to reflect her state of readiness.

Orion was unique in his presence and demeanor, indicative of his otherworldliness. She was used to her spirit friends who came from higher realms in the spirit world but with Orion, the difference was palpable. This didn't scare her, nor was it uncomfortable. She felt his love for her and Jeremy, and this feeling always gave her a sense that all was well when she opened herself up to spirit communication. He also was not a spirit in the true sense of someone being discarnate. He had a body which lay in repose on his home planet, lovingly cared for by attendants well versed in such things. Orion was not alone in his attempts to communicate with earthlings. He had an entire team of helpers and assistants who ensured that he was both safe and capable of carrying out his desire to forge a bond with his friends on Earth. Contact was made in an instant of thought as he homed in on Sadie's spiritual signature. Sadie had only known spirits who did not have corporal bodies, who were dead to the material world. Orion, however, was still alive and this intrigued her greatly. She was excited to have him come and speak through her and so it began.

"Greetings to you my friends, I am Orion and very pleased that you have some time in your day to facilitate our communication," said Orion in a deep and authoritative voice. "I am happy that we will begin a series of communications that will include questions which you may formulate and speak out loud as we talk. This instrument is well equipped to sustain a rapport with me for an extended period of time, and I suggest that we spend an hour in these sessions to thoroughly explore various subjects together."

"We will start rather slowly, allowing us all to adjust and settle into the rhythm of this form of communication. There is nothing that you cannot ask of me, Jeremy. I am willing to answer as many questions as you can formulate to the best of my ability. Of course, we are limited by the capacity of mediumship to give full, even technical responses to you. Thus, we will be somewhat generalized in our answers. This is best, because even if we did not have these restrictions, your capacity to understand deeper concepts of universal truth are also hampered by your mind's biases and constrictions of thought. Do you have any questions for me now Jeremy?" Jeremy felt a pang of inadequacy mixed with fear that he would ask a stupid question to this obviously advanced intellect. "I can't think of anything at the moment which would be up to the standards of the opportunity that you have offered," Jeremy blurted out with the slight stutter of anxiety.

Orion gave a little laugh as he considered Jeremy's response. "Dear boy, there is no need to be self-conscious with me. There is no question that I would consider to be unworthy or inappropriate. I am here to educate, inform, and inspire you both. We will also give to your world a story like no other, something which we hope will help to set humanity's sights toward higher thought and aspirations. There is so much potential within you, Jeremy and within humanity. Your race sits upon the cusp of great change, an evolutionary leap, provided you are able to overcome the impediments of your human condition. The time is now to act, deciding your fate and the fate of generations to come. Thus, we place upon you dear friend a great responsibility and a gift, something to help guide your brothers and sisters to the truth about themselves and about their fate. No small task, I know, but one I believe you and your cohort are up to. We have waited a long time for this opportunity. The igniting of two dear and gifted souls in collaboration with us to open the doorway to many things yet unimagined or known," said Orion

Once again, Jeremy began to doubt himself. He was beginning to understand the implications of what Orion was saying, but as he did so, a deep sense of inadequacy rose up from his gut "How could I take on something like this?" he said with a sense of urgency and fear. "I've never desired anything more than a life that is quiet and uncomplicated," Jeremy shared with the transformed figure of Sadie overshadowed by the unmistakable other presence of Orion. "I think that you have the wrong man, since I don't possess a deep intellect or any great ambitions to be a leader, not to mention one who could share such a message. I'm a nobody," he concluded in a plaintive tone.

"Yes, you are a nobody as you say my friend and that is why we have chosen you for the task," Orion confided with the deepest respect and love.

"Nobodies are anonymous, humble, and often lack ambition. Thus, you represent someone who can be taught, trained and developed into an effective instrument for our cause. It is not that you will lose your identity, or unable to find your equilibrium in the unfolding of this daring plan. Rather, you will be added to, enhanced and ultimately find deep satisfaction and meaning as the journey unfolds. No one involved here will suffer from loss in any way. Rather, you will come to know parts of yourself that you never thought existed, gifts that will astound you, and abilities that will prove that you are up to the task," Orion stated with a power of persuasion that left no room for argument.

"You are a babe in the woods, and your confusion and lack of confidence is understandable. It will take time to find your feet and come to understand these things. Patience and forbearance is your friend as you move forward. I implore you not to let go of your initial enthusiasm. Instead, look toward what can be rather than your perceived inadequacies. You must see yourself in good hands and have faith in your future with us," Orion concluded.

Jeremy didn't know what to say. He was filled with conflicting thoughts and emotions. On one hand, he was enthralled by the prospect of new adventures and possible outcomes never before imagined. On the other hand, he was all too aware of his deep-seated doubts and fears.

Oh, what a dilemma Orion presented him with, sensing the air of expectancy filling the room.

"I think that we should end our session now," Orion wisely suggested, "There are things that need further consideration since the road ahead has become clearer to you. We cannot coerce you into anything, Jeremy. It requires agreement from all parties concerned. As for me and this dear soul before you, the pact is already sealed. Thus, it requires your approval now and I can see that you are too conflicted to come to a reasonable decision. Take your time, Jeremy and decide when you have weighed all the options. I'm sure that when you see what a marvelous opportunity that has been presented to you, you will choose with wisdom and grace," said Orion with an air of detachment.

With that, Sadie gave a great sigh, indicating that Orion was gone and Sadie was present once again. It took her a few minutes to come back from a place that seemed far away. Jeremy noticed that her eyes were no longer dilated, having that unusual gaze that was indicative of Orion's presence. Rather, she was now herself, looking at him somewhat quizzically as she regained her composure.

"Wasn't that interesting?" she said with a bit of wonder. "I rarely go that deep. Usually, I'm half here and can even hear the words spoken, sort of like stepping back a bit and giving up my mind and body to the spirit who is speaking," she confided.

"This time I went deep and for what seemed like hours. I can't tell you how well rested I feel, as she gave a slight yawn."

"What was it like for you Jeremy? "

"I can't really say in a few words Sadie," Jeremy blurted out with a combination of bewilderment laced with fear. "He said a lot of things which I have to think about and consider for the future," said Jeremy, giving Sadie a plaintive look. "Well, I can't spend a lot of time with you right now Jeremy, as I have other things to do," she said, regaining her usual curt manner. "We'll have to chat next time. Next Tuesday then?" she asked without hearing his answer.

They both rose from their seats and he headed for the door. As he left, Sadie said something odd. "You know, I've always felt alone in this life because most people don't understand what I do. I know that they think of me as a witch or some such thing that is just as unflattering. I feel a strong bond and kinship with you Jeremy. We can do great things together, you and I. Please don't shirk from this opportunity. We need one another, and that isn't something I have said to someone for a very long time."

At that, Jeremy nodded and closed the door behind him. He never felt more alone despite Sadie's reassurances. He hated complications and this was by far the most complicated situation he had ever encountered. Oh, how life can throw you a curveball when you least expect it, he mused as he made his way home, seeking the comfort of familiar surroundings. It was like leaving a different world behind and coming back to reality. How odd it all felt, yet intriguing and hopeful. So much to think about and he was glad that he had his work, friends, and dog to ground him from his bizarre experience with Sadie and Orion.

Chapter 12

FINDING HOME

Unfortunately, Jeremy had to miss his next appointment with Sadie. This worried her as she knew that he was not the sort of person to renege on his commitments. She tried phoning him but he did not answer. She tried reaching out to him psychically using their shared bond as a way of connecting, but this too proved fruitless. Although she didn't like leaving her home and the protection that it afforded her, she decided to go and visit him where he lived.

It was a Sunday morning and she knew that Jeremy would be home. She drove up in her ancient Volkswagen Beetle, coughing and sputtering her way into town with a blue trail of smoke tracing her route. Some people stopped and stared as she passed. Sadie was well known around town but few had seen her out and about in this neck of the woods. This was a novelty — no doubt to be discussed at the local coffee shop later in the week. There was talk about Sadie and Jeremy having an affair since his truck was seen regularly outside her home. Speculation and rumors swirled around town, but nothing was ever verified other than some circumstantial evidence. Since Jeremy lived in a central location, more than one busybody saw Sadie pull up to his house and go in. Knowing looks were shared among the neighbors as she did so — big news in such a small place.

Sadie knocked on Jeremy's door loudly and insistently. Jeremy was having his morning coffee out back, but he could hear her knocking from where he was sitting. He quickly got up to see who was there. He didn't have many visitors so he thought that this must be something important. As he opened the door, a look of both panic and surprise filled his expression so that even someone who was not psychic could read it clearly.

"Sssss...adie," he stammered as the color in his face noticeably reddened, "What are you doing here?" he managed to say without stumbling over his words.

"Since you won't come to see me young man, I've come to see you. So can I come in?" she asked with a look of both expectancy and consternation.

Jeremy's eyes widened as he opened the door for her to enter. All the while looking up and down the block to see who was out on the street. He saw more than a few neighbors chatting and casting their gaze in his direction. Thoughts of future inquiries flit through his mind as he let her in. He felt like he was in trouble as Sadie moved to the living room and plunked herself down.

"Are you going to offer your visitor a cup of tea or are you so not used to entertaining that you have forgotten your manners?" piercing him with an accusatory look.

"Oooo...h, of course, Sadie, what would you like?" he said with a tinge of guilt.

"You know what I like, a bit of black tea with milk would be fine. And if you have a biscuit or something sweet to go with it, I would appreciate it since I haven't had anything to eat today. "

He scurried to the kitchen to fill her order. Rex was there with a quizzical look on his face, accompanied by a whine of concern. He knew Sadie, smelling the cat scent that was so much a part of her presence. He sensed that she was not a threat, but not welcome either. Jeremy put his hand on Rex and said some reassuring words, promising that they would head out soon on their usual Sunday adventure. Rex lay down on his mat with a plaintive groan but stayed put while Jeremy prepared the snack for Sadie.

Her tea was presented in the only teacup that he owned —a keepsake that was given to him when his grandmother died. After giving it a thorough rinsing out, he poured the tea and applied the milk in just the way that Sadie taught him. He had a few cookies which he put on the rim of the saucer and walked out to the living room, presenting his peace offering in such a polite way that his mother would surely be proud. The room was neat and tidy since he didn't really use it much, preferring to eat and watch his TV in a small, converted back bedroom.

He settled into an armchair opposite Sadie's and began, "I'm sorry that I missed our appointment, Sadie. Work is so busy right now and I plum forgot. I'm flattered that you would come all this way in order to see if I'm OK and as you can see, I am."

Sadie said nothing, allowing him more rope to hang himself before she set him straight.

"As I told you last time we met, Orion put a big ask on me, something I was not prepared for and it put me in a bit of a tailspin. I still haven't figured out what I'm going to do. I don't like complications in my life and this Orion thing is far more complicated than I would like," Jeremy concluded while taking another slurp out of his now cold coffee.

Sadie couldn't hold back any longer. "You are a coward Jeremy Flynn." her eyes ablaze with accusation. "I thought that you were better than that, but you proved me wrong. You are like most of them out there. You prefer to allow life to pass you by in your usual somnambulist state. Wake up Jeremy," she almost pleaded. "A great opportunity has been laid at your feet and all you can think about is your creature comforts and desire to not be challenged by life. This is pathetic and I wonder why I even bothered coming over here in order to hear you give lame excuses and outright lies. I thought you were my friend Jeremy. Friends don't lie to one another, nor do they shirk their responsibilities and commitments to one another. It appears that you are comfortable doing both," eyes still ablaze, her hands slightly trembling as she took a sip of her tea to calm down.

Jeremy thought that he had never met such a fierce and unusual woman as Sadie Jenkins — bold enough to come into his home and give him such a dressing down. Yet, underneath this hard exterior was a woman who clearly cared for him. She had spent so much time giving and nurturing him in many ways. She was wise and at times very gentle, such an enigma.

Almost tearing up, Jeremy apologized for his bad behavior. He was ashamed of himself and felt deep remorse, though everything that he had experienced in the last while was so new and out of place for him that he needed to step back and reassess. He told Sadie as much and asked for forgiveness.

Sadie shouted, "I don't want your apologies Jeremy," loud enough for his curious neighbors to hear. "I need your loyalty and commitment to something that is far bigger than you or I. I forgive you if that's what you are looking for, but I can't be kept waiting for you to resolve your ambivalence. I need to know one way or another. At least you owe us, Orion and I, the courtesy of making up your mind."

She couldn't have put it more clearly. It was a do-or-die moment, and he knew that if he didn't decide right now, he would lose his best friend and, no doubt, return to the somnambulistic state that Sadie described. This was a turning point for him. He needed to be shaken up by the truth about his passivity and lack of backbone. More shame crept in as he contemplated his past. He knew that if he didn't overcome these impediments, he would live to regret it for the rest of his life. There and then, he resolved to change his ways and to be true to what he was and can be as a man with honor, dignity, and courage.

The dam had burst, and Jeremy dissolved into tears, slumping into Sadie's arms as he released those long-held burdens of fear and self-loathing. As he sobbed while muttering his regrets, soaking Sadie's shoulder, she held on and poured out the sweetness of her soul in gentle understanding and affirmation of what a beautiful soul he is. This went on for quite some time and as Jeremy emerged from his cathartic state, he felt lighter with a clear head and an open heart. He was ready to continue with the work that had been presented. A new resolve welled up from within as he pledged his support to both Sadie and Orion there and then. Sadie couldn't be more pleased.

"So, we'll see you at our appointed hour next week", giving him a steady gaze that indicated that she meant business!

"Yes Sadie," said Jeremy as he regained some composure. "I'll be there, and I want you to know that I'm not a coward. I'm just a bit scared and I'm the cautious type. But once I make up my mind, I'm 100% there. You can count on that!"

With these words, Sadie picked herself off the sagging couch and headed home, not yet finishing her tea and stale cookies. Even more neighbors were on the lawn now, having heard the exchange half a block away. The old witch was out of her lair, harassing poor Jeremy. Tisk, tisk muttered the busy bodies.

Since the show was over, many onlookers retreated to their homes, shaking their heads in wonder. Little did they know that something truly extraordinary had been born with this dramatic exchange — nor would they ever know, since their knowledge and capacity to understand were so different from the worlds that both Jeremy and Sadie were about to explore. They both knew that they would be the subject of prurient conversations and distorted judgments, but their focus was on the journey ahead! What the world thought of them was of no true concern. They were outliers in a community concerned about petty differences rather than matters far beyond the mundane. The chasm was huge and as time progressed, it would become insurmountable.

Chapter 13

A New Start

Jeremy entered Sadie's home with a renewed sense of purpose and enthusiasm. Gone were the doubts and fears of the past. He practically leapt through the door as Sadie bid him to enter. With a smile on his face and an eagerness that he hadn't felt since childhood, Jeremy sat down at his designated chair, brushing aside her beloved cat, George. He wasn't really a cat person but today he felt a love for the big Tabby that made the cat purr in appreciation. He felt like he belonged there, like family, and it felt good.

Sadie too was in a good mood, reassured by Jeremy's turnaround in attitude and prompt arrival —an auspicious new beginning. They began their session with a prayer. Sadie never said the same prayer twice; rather, she spoke of what was in her head and heart at the time. Sending the desires of her soul heavenward

So she began, "Oh Lord of the universe, source of all love, be with us today as we embark on new beginnings and help us to renew our commitment to the highest and best outcomes for our work. Please know that we love you, and we desire to be blessed by your touch of love, divine love, within our souls. We also ask that we may be blessed with the presence of angels and our stellar friend Orion. Bring us into the light of your grace and open us up to divine purpose. Thank you beloved God, amen."

As Sadie concluded her prayer, she once again fell into a deep trance and welcomed Orion, who spoke his greetings. — "My friends. I am here. I am Orion. Yes, the world of distractions swirls around you both. A world filled with many aspects of stimulation, thoughts, conditions, feelings that are not in harmony with a peaceful soul. Thus, at times it is difficult for me to penetrate these conditions and to be with you as clearly as I might.

"Yet here I am with you today. We will continue in this endeavor to work on this project — an effort to bring greater truth and information forward so that many may understand and know what it is to be an inhabitant of the great universe of divine creation. I am ready to receive your questions and do my best to answer through an instrument that has certain limitations. Therefore, the details and complexity of my answers may not be readily expressed. We may begin."

Jeremy had prepared this time and began to deliver his questions for Orion's consideration.

Jeremy

"Can you verify that you are who you say you are and that you come from another planet? I think it is important to have verification before we begin."

Orion

"This is a somewhat amusing question, as you have had several encounters with me before this time. These encounters were quite unique, filled with experiences that could not be had by any other means than through my influence and presence with you. The human mind is a suspicious creature. Everything that goes through this mind is often distorted and treated with suspicion. Your earthly reality is created by this mind and all its faculties. It is not true reality that is part of the universal reality known by many not of your world. Rather, it is a construct that has been carefully crafted over millennia of human experience. Therefore, accepting something outside of these parameters can be difficult for any individual who lives upon your Earth. Yet, you have come together with the hope that indeed these constructs will be shattered, and something fresh, new, and powerful may come in its stead.

"We are eager, hoping that all parties may work together to bring, not another creation of the mind but the reality and truth of life that stretches far beyond this small planet. You never seem to fully overcome your human traits of doubt, Jeremy, rather you have moments of lucidity bringing fragments of understanding and inspiration, interrupted, and disturbed by the humanness that resides within you. Therefore, you struggle with the possibilities of what can be, and you possess a secret desire that these possibilities will fit into your present paradigm of thought.

"Yet, how can what I have to offer fit into such a limited paradigm? It is impossible because you wish to make me a human, an individual who resides upon the Earth, or at the very least, a being that may be false and acting under false pretenses in order to draw you into some nefarious scheme or idea concocted by them. This too is folly. We must overcome these things as we continue in this venture so that you and those you may share my words with, may be reassured that I am indeed real. That I reside on a different planet than yourself, that I come from very far away— so far away, that even with your most sophisticated telescopes, you couldn't see the planet on which I reside.

"The Milky Way galaxy is large, consisting of many spirals, aspects and quadrants within it that are far beyond the sight of humanity despite its present technologies. The distance that I might cover between where I reside in the flesh and have come here in my spirit body is so immense that it would take thousands of light-years to traverse. I come by thought, by my capacities and development of my spirit body and my soul in order to readily accomplish this connection between us."

Jeremy
"How is it possible to travel in this way? "

Orion

"The capacities to do this are inherent in our development as a race. This development is not exclusive to us because it can be accomplished by all of humanity, I say humanity because from my perspective you and I are brothers as we are related, a part of the great universe of humanity. Indeed, each expression of that race upon different planets and different iterations of humanity upon these planets follow templates and patterns that are continuously repeated within the universe. Thus, all of humanity is capable of this as well, though the latency of the capacities to travel in this way is extremely limited by your lack of soul development. Therefore, humanity is not able to understand these concepts well. Yet, there are within you and within all in the universe many potentials and capacities that can be developed once the soul, that true core that is you, is developed so its faculties and capacities may be expressed and utilized for such a thing as interstellar travel.

"The capacity to travel is within a blink of an eye. It is a thought; it is a desire to move from one place to another. There are many layers upon your world beside this physical one, there are beings who inhabit higher levels of consciousness than yours. They understand such concepts and use them quite readily. We have been contacted by these higher beings who live on spirit levels that are far beyond this one, but still part of the Earth. Our ability to connect and be here has been facilitated by these beings, those who have developed greatly in their spirit life, a life that is situated far beyond this physical plane."

Jeremy

"So you say that your main goal in coming here on Earth is to try and teach us to progress in our souls so that we can develop these capacities? Don't some use spaceships? Do you use spaceships?"

Orion

"I will answer the last question first. We have the ways and means of transportation within vehicles that would carry our physical bodies. We have the ways and means of materializing and dematerializing these vehicles. So yes, we do have spaceships as you call them. They are operated in a way that utilizes multi-dimensional travel where time and space are not relevant. We may travel yet again in instantaneous ways that would astound you. For the purpose of what we are doing here together, however, there is no need for a vehicle.—only the need for me as an entity and consciousness to connect with you both. We do not require a physical presence at this time. There may come a time when we will make our presence known in a physical way. There have been others, other races from other planets, who have made contact in this way. Although this is a very confusing matter for humanity, as governments and other powers do not wish for these things to be known or validated at present. Indeed, in some respects, it is a wise decision because humanity is not ready to truly understand the nature of the cosmos and the nature of their brothers and sisters who are beyond the reach of this planet but who visit and observe you."

Jeremy

"Can they be trusted? All the sightings, are they also beings of a higher progression?"

Orion

"There is a law in the universe that such capacities and abilities cannot be developed and entertained unless there is a high degree of moral, spiritual, and emotional development within that race. In this way, the universe ensures that humanity is separated one from another until that time comes when they have matured enough to be able to make contact in a way that does not bring mutual harm.

"There are many speculations on your planet about the nature and capacities of these beings. Indeed, many stories and ideas have arisen from extraterrestrial contact with individuals upon your planet. There are deep suspicions and fears in humanity. Indeed, the ability of the individual to truly experience with clarity these encounters is highly unlikely. Many are given the opportunity to encounter these benevolent beings and they come away with their minds confused and feeling that somehow they are threatened and have been violated.

"This is not the truth. Those things that come as stories of violations and behaviors that are unloving are concoctions of the human mind, fabrications designed to misdirect the truth of such contacts. It reflects the efforts of some to disrupt and disturb the intentions of these benevolent beings. It creates barriers and fears between humanity and those who would make contact. It is unfortunate because these beings cannot cause harm. They do not intend to conquer or enslave humanity as humanity fears. This is a projection of human thought and deep speculation in order to make sense of these unusual experiences. These beings come to bring what they can to help uplift humanity. Humanity has many problems and dilemmas that need attention and solutions.

"Unfortunately, humanity is unable to use the resources and mental capacities that they possess to solve these dilemmas. Your economies are dysfunctional and centered upon an individual's accumulation of wealth and power. Sadly, the motivation to heal the planet and those upon it is weak and ineffective. There are many who have the desire, but those in power do not see it as a priority. The dysfunctions, damage, and ruination of your planet continue to escalate. This is the reason for our interventions and efforts in whatever way that might manifest for the good of all.

"Yet, we are discredited, we are disbelieved, we are feared, and we are made into something that we are not. Your science fiction movies and imaginations reflecting the human condition continue to portray us as the enemy, one who wishes destruction, manipulation, and who is detached and unloving. The lack of truth is indeed a frustrating reality for us, interfering with what we might bring to help you from the intense suffering that you all endure. Yet, the back and forth of speculation and experience continues to play out in many different ways. Though humanity is slowly coming to the realization that they are not alone, it is fraught with many speculations which contaminate the thoughts of humanity."

Jeremy
"How long have you been watching me and why are you watching me, and why me?"

Orion
"My beloved friend, you have a purity about you that is uncommon in your world. You are a unique individual and have a fortunate combination of gifts of personality and motivation that make you a prime candidate for our venture together. We have scoured the Earth for such individuals and there are a few but we have found an ideal match with you and this instrument. We have conspired to bring you together and accomplish much as the three of us continue to forge an important alliance.

"My first encounter with you was intended to open up your mind to the possibilities of what may be. I know that this approach was startling and difficult for you, but it produced the results intended. We know you well, Jeremy. My mind is quite capable of knowing your mind as we are telepathically connected. We are together — friends and cohorts in something that I hope will bring valuable information to the world, something that is needed for humanity to take those next steps beyond the constrictions of the human condition.

"We come together because you are a necessary component to this venture. You have within you many capacities to understand, see, visualize, integrate, and be open to what is offered. We are together and we will find our way upon a journey that will be both intense and rewarding. You will encounter many things through this relationship that very few on Earth have experienced. So we continue. I have taken my time in order to make contact with you, but here we are and here we shall continue to travel upon a path resplendent with beauty and possibility."

Jeremy
"What do you want me to do?"

Orion
"You are doing what I want you to do, dear Jeremy. You are walking with me for a time, with us both in close connection and harmony together. I have many things to impart to you so that you may, in time, may impart these things to others.

Jeremy
Me?

Orion
"Yes you, my friend. You do not understand the gifts that lay within you. With your limited thinking you see yourself as an average, humble individual living a very average life. Yet beyond that understanding is a soul that has many capacities, a soul which I mentioned earlier that can manifest many abilities and gifts that would astound you at this time.

Part of our journey together is to help develop these capacities within you.

"First and foremost, you must understand what a soul requires to be nurtured and to come alive. There is universal energy that is capable of awakening you. Your dear friend calls this God's love, the divine love. This is as good a name as any. For it does spring forth from the divine Creator, source of all love. It is an substance that you are capable of absorbing given your understanding of its existence.

"To begin with, you must seek this love. Seek the elixir of the soul of God. This is what empowers all of humanity throughout the universe, but it is given through free will. It does not come as an automatic part of your being upon birth. Love certainly exists there, a love that is human, but this is different from of love."

Jeremy

"Is that what I feel when I am with Sadie, and when you come?"

Orion

Indeed you do, indeed you do! I am greatly empowered with this energy, this universal love and so is your friend who has been receiving it for some time. This capacity to foster our connection has come about because of your dear friend's light. Her beautiful soul has brought me close; consequently, I have brought you close and into this fold of love. It is my wish for you to experience this blessing and to grow within it. We may accomplish many things together as you seek the empowerment of love that can create many beautiful things.

Jeremy

"May I ask how old you are?"

Orion

"In your terms, I am ancient. I have lived in the physical body for several hundred Earth years. We live on a planet that is so infused with the energies of the Divine that our life span is greatly enhanced. In time, your Earth will be able to sustain human life for a very long time. Of course, your planet will have to go through great adjustments. You are vastly overpopulated. Our planet has two to three billion souls residing within it at one time. This is sufficient to create a harmonious environment for us and for all life upon it."

Jeanne

"And now we have eight billion on Earth."

Orion

"Yes, you now have many, many souls inhabiting your Earth, many of them living in difficult and impoverished situations, while others live a life so rich with material goods and experiences that this imbalance is causing great distress to your Earth and to everyone upon it. A very unfortunate condition indeed, one that we see will be rectified soon enough."

Jeremy

"Have you seen other planets that struggle like we do?"

Orion

"Yes, there are several planets that must evolve in this way. Humanity made a choice at the beginning of its existence to evolve in a certain direction. It is a hard road that has been chosen, a road that continually reinforces the empowerment of humans and diminishes the empowerment of God. Even when God is invoked, it is through religions and concepts that are a reflection of a desire for power and control. On our planet, we understand the laws of creation, the laws of the universe. We are happy to be in partnership with the great Creator of the universe in order to continue on a journey of further development, further harmony with God and with the universe. We are humble in our approach, honoring God for what God is while recognizing our place in the cosmos at the same time. We are here with you to help you take such a journey, to help you to understand what that journey entails, to help you to see the way forward."

Jeremy

"Do you know the angels Sadie knows? Do you work with them? How did you.....I don't understand."

Orion

"These beautiful beings, who call themselves Celestial Angels, have made contact with us and us with them. They are the same angels in which our dear Sadie has encountered and continues to encounter. There is great harmony here, a plan, a way forward that will open up many others to the possibilities of life and the existence of such beings. Many will come to realize the gradations of life that bring greater harmony and greater capacity to exist in light, harmony, and a loving condition rather than that of the great deprivation which exists now upon your planet."

Jeremy

I don't know how you're going to make this happen because we can't even tell anybody about you. After all, they won't believe us. They think bad things about Sadie and I don't see how this is possible."

Orion

"You have a saying: Here, but for the Grace of God, go I. Indeed, but for the grace of God I am here. God has a plan that encompasses the universe. All of creation is part of a great plan, a great trajectory toward harmony, toward greater development, and toward awakening. Indeed, I am here because I have been called and I have been inspired by the Creator to come to your planet to help to facilitate this plan. Of course, I am not the only one involved. There are many, many individuals involved in this great plan. Thus, the small work that we do together can be magnified in many ways through others and through the efforts made to help bring truth to humanity.

"Humanity is on the cusp of something great, but humanity is in great danger as well. Humanity continues to entertain many dark and nefarious acts and trends that have the possibility of bringing death to all. God intervenes. Within God's great compassion for humanity, many efforts are made to help neutralize these conditions, reversing the course of human endeavor toward that which is more harmonious. Thus, the ability to understand and realize the truth of their existence must come to the consciousness of humanity. Otherwise, humanity will not endure nor thrive. Humanity will perish. I am part of a mission of mercy, a mission to help save the human race from its own impetus toward oblivion."

Jeremy

"This is so hard to understand because it doesn't seem like God's interventions are working at all. There are more wars, and we can't stop it. I don't see what God is doing is very powerful. I'm sorry to say this, but I just don't understand."

Orion

"Free will is one of the most powerful gifts given to humanity. All of humanity in the universe has free will. Humanity through its expression of free will has determined a certain trajectory of development. Free will is not the only force in play here. There is the divine force and there are those actors within that divine flow that are working to bring harmony to the Earth. Many of them are in the spirit world, but there are some on the Earth plane such as you.

"Our endeavors may begin small and, in your mind, ineffectual, but the momentum will build. We are engaged in building light, truth, communication, and greater harmony. You cannot see the capacities and probabilities of what this endeavor may bring. You need patience and faith in what may come of these efforts.

"My friend, our hope is that you may see the beginning of something tremendous and powerful, something beyond your imagination. We do not know what God has planned to any great degree, but we know that we are part of something that is far greater, more intricate and involved than even I can know. We step forward in faith and we will continue to step forward.

"I believe we should finish our interview and come back another time to engage again in this way. There is indeed much to consider in what I have said. I urge you, my dear friend, to take what we have said seriously and to ruminate upon it, opening your mind to the possibilities. I also urge you to engage in prayer often so that you may receive this gift from God, — this essence, so you may grow within this part of you that you do not know well enough as yet..

"I extend my blessings to you, my friend — blessings to you both. We will meet again."

Jeremy

"Thank you, Orion. The enormity is great. I will see you another time. Thank you."

Jeremy returned to his normal mindset, feeling the overwhelming weight of the responsibility that had been placed upon him. Orion had laid things out as clearly as he could. The seriousness of the matter was not to be missed, and he knew that what he was being enlisted to do would not be easy or enjoyable despite Orion's encouragement. If Orion was right, then the fate of the world rested on his shoulders although he knew that others were a part of a very large plan to rescue humanity from their own twisted and dangerous ambitions and desires.

This is not what he expected. He imagined that he was going to be part of a personal journey that would resolve a lot of questions he had about life, both personal and general. He knew that this would be true, but the price that was to be paid for knowing the truth would be his compliance as an instrument of change that was tremendous in scope. In his gut, he knew that everything had changed in his life. He was no longer part of a world that normalized everything and did not tolerate disruption of the shared illusion, which could ultimately steer humanity toward its ultimate destruction. In this reality, there was no need to make any effort outside of being another cog in a very large system. — one too large to comprehend or stop. He was about to embark on a process of ripping away illusions and seeing the truth. This scared and excited him at the same time, plunging full speed ahead towards the unknown.

Chapter 14

ONE STEP AT A TIME

Jeremy wanted to share his new insights and experiences with the world. His friends and family were both equally intrigued and concerned for his present state of mind. He seemed happy enough, if not a little pensive, continuing with his regular routines as normal. It was obvious to most that Jeremy was captivated by his new focus on life. Mrs. Phelps surmised that Jeremy would get over this newfound fad in time. Michael was more than worried. He felt abandoned by his best friend. It was almost as if he was witnessing Jeremy's decline into some sort of psychosis. It was clear that he had lost it and was oblivious to what was happening around him.

Jeremy's descriptions of what happened at Sadie's house fit the mold of town gossip and speculation. Yet Jeremy spoke in the most loving terms about Sadie and had no compunction to tell all about their unusual friendship and project. Since his last visit, Jeremy felt elated. He experienced a palpable sense of joy burning in his chest and a renewed faith and awareness of God, reflecting an inner sense of God's love for him. It defied reason, yet he knew beyond doubt that he was on the road to salvation. Not salvation in a biblical sense, but one that gave him such a sense of freedom and expansion that he knew in his bones was true and real.

Boy, you couldn't make this up, thought Jeremy with an inner chuckle. Yet, he wasn't afraid to share his story with those close to him. He told his mother and sister about some of his experiences at their last Sunday dinner together. They shared looks of incredulity and horror with one another, but Jeremy was oblivious to their response. He was happy to share and revel in his newfound perspective with no concern for his mother's or sister's shock and dismay. Both thought that he had lost his mind, but, like others, could not detect anything wrong with him. Instead, he seemed happier than either of them had ever seen him.

His life had been reset, giving him renewed purpose and a sense of joy, just as Orion had predicted. He wondered how long this would last, fully expecting something to happen to knock him back into the emotional doldrums. Although his mind was overwhelmed with caution, red flags and doubts refuting his experiences with Sadie and Orion, he also felt as if the hand of God was on him and it felt wonderful.

Jeremy's next meeting at Sadie's was full of warmth and good cheer. It was like having Christmas in July. Her demeanor towards him had softened considerably and the two of them kibitzed like school children on the playground. Sadie was relieved to see Jeremy so relaxed and happy. Upon hearing about his budding connection with God, she felt relieved, happy that Jeremy had truly learned about the power of divine love. Her fervent hope was that he would rocket towards true soul ascension and transformation by applying this truth to his life.

As their allotted time approached, each was eager to start. Sadie, as always, said her opening prayer, invoking the highest blessings from God, with hopes their special friend Orion might speak to them today.

No sooner had Sadie finished her invocation, Orion showed up right on cue and began to speak

"I am Orion. You have asked why we are here and our purpose might be for being here. Indeed, if you could see the world as we see your world, it is obvious that it is in great need of support, guidance, and love. Your world is frenetic and chaotic, filled with billions upon billions of individuals seeking self-gratification and engagement in the material sense. With such fear and dysfunction existing on Earth, the possibilities of conflict, wars, circumstances of deprivation, and pain are far more prevalent than those of love and harmony.

"We are a species of love and harmony. We have learned to live in this way for a far greater time than humanity has been on this planet. There is no conflict on our planet. There is no need to compete for resources and material gain as we are quite refined in our spiritual being. We require less input and effort in order to maintain ourselves. We do not require much material sustenance or the safety of a physical structure. Rather, because of our spiritual gain and enlightenment, we are able to fabricate with our mind's structures and material items so that our life is more fluid in its expressions. We do utilize some material resources in order to manifest things in a material way, but the impact of our endeavors is small and almost negligible.

"We do not need to build imposing edifices and structures like you require. Our children do not go to school as every day provides them with the opportunity to learn and to grow. We do not have hospitals since we have no need for such things. Our bodies are sustained for several hundred years because of our planet's atmosphere, combined with our body's DNA, and spiritual refinement conspires to sustain us in every way. The way we live and interact is very different from your own world. Yet, we are compelled to reach out to those on other planets who are in trouble, who require guidance and are in need of upliftment from the quagmire of their own conditions created by ignorance and unfortunate choices.

"There is a constant in the universe, and it is that all beings who possess a soul, intelligence, and ability to move in the material universe are gifted with free will. They can choose their fate, as you have chosen yours. Because of this powerful gift, it is quite possible for humans to choose between creating hell or heaven on Earth. These conditions are the result of an untold multitude of choices made every day among billions of souls. This great collective of thought and deed creates ebbs and flows of energetic and physical influence that affect the collective consciousness of humans.

"We observe these energies building and being transferred from one to another until currents of thought and deed become powerful beyond your imaginings. The world is made up of many choices reflecting actions, beliefs, and thoughts that are accepted as truth and create the reality of men. These things continue to forge the components that can lead you down a path of self-destruction.

"As beings attuned to God, the laws of the universe, and a deepening understanding of how the laws function; how can we stand by and watch those whom we consider our brothers and sisters slip down this terrible slope? It is a path that few understand or realize they are creating daily in their thoughts and actions. Intervention is required and so we are here to help gather those resources needed to bring change and healing for your planet

"We understand that life goes on, that indeed if all of humanity lost their ability to live upon this Earth, they would still have the capacity to live in the spirit world although the loss of the material plane would disallow further incarnations of souls. This too contradicts the laws of creation which dictate continuous development and manifestation in God's great universe. This means that the law of regeneration which requires physical procreation must exist in life. Humanity, as with every being within the universe, has the equivalent of a duplicate body that lives on. We have been able to integrate these two bodies, both the material and the spiritual, while we live on our planet in such a way that we are not so reliant upon the physical necessities as you are.

"Besides possessing a spirit body it is important to recognize the most crucial and capable aspect of myself, my soul. We call this 'the flame of life' for without a soul, we could not exist. It is the fundamental essence of who we are. And, astonishingly, each soul in the universe is unique.

There are no two alike even though we are all created as binary beings, usually in the form of one female and one male. This is a fundamental and universal attribute of all souls. Each is separated upon incarnation into physical form. They are destined to reunite as self-contained and developed humans. The soul has many qualities which can be readily recognized as expressions of love, wisdom, and perception. Each soul has a storehouse of gifts or abilities that are ignited when the soul comes into a state of wakefulness. Soon, I will explain the process of awakening to you so that you might understand it in more detail. For now, it is better for you to understand your true nature as you exist presently before we discuss more complex issues pertaining to a soul's development and progression. We all possess a soul Jeremy, and because of this kinship, we are brothers and sisters in God's Universe. In time, you will be able to perceive your own soul's potential and recognize its characteristics. It is crucial that you do so because, without this awareness, we cannot proceed with your education to any great degree. The success of our venture relies on your investment in time, thought, and application towards what we will share with you soon .

"There comes a time, even for us, when we must transition into the next dimension of life. It is a longer lifespan than yours, far longer. It is a joyous life, a full life, one that allows us many explorations, and many capacities to communicate with other species, other beings that live on planets in our shared universe. The interchange and interactions between us is rich and full. We also serve others by assisting those of you who are spiritually and physically in need of greater knowledge and understanding so that they may find universal truths that can be applied for their benefit. We come gently, so you do not know us. We do not appear in some flying saucer, as you call it, and land upon the lawn of the houses of power and government like some fanciful science fiction movie. Rather, we work with individuals such as yourself. We work with many trying to influence and uphold them, to lead them upon a path that is in harmony with the laws of the universe rather than one that is chaotic and lacks structure and harmony with them.

"Here we are together communicating. I know you would prefer that I continue to materialize in front of you and speak to you. But this is not how we wish to approach our communications. In time, my friend, at the right time, we will indeed materialize and show ourselves, as will many others. This will be a time of great trepidation, excitement and hope. But the time is not now. This is a time of preparation, of laying the foundations, of teaching those who will listen about the true nature of life, the laws of life in a way that everyone can understand and adopt. Rather than make these laws into dogma and edicts, we will offer our teachings in the form of invitation and demonstration. In this way, all people will be given the opportunity of choice to accept or reject what is given. Harmony is important to us and we are intent on living under the laws of harmony in all that we do.

"What I will say to you, my dear friend, is only truth given clearly and succinctly as we can under these circumstances. It will be a journey filled with wonders. When we complete this journey, I hope that you will be enlightened and awakened to the possibilities of your being, understanding how it will come and knowing the way to proceed. I will be your teacher. I hope that you will be my student so that we can proceed in harmony, love, and respect for one another.

"You have seen me. You know that I exist. You have traveled with me and know that where I come from exists. You need to overcome your fears, speculations, and judgments in order to come to a reasonable state of understanding of one another, so we proceed as true friends. It requires a bond of love for us to sustain this condition and opportunity for communication.

"I ask you, my friend, are you willing to commit yourself in the ways that we have asked? Can you truly believe that what is happening between us is real, as real as anything in your life? In the reality that we share, much truth, understanding, and wisdom will come, and you will become a changed person. You will be an active participant and, as my student, you will become a teacher.

"This is a great opportunity, an invitation that may change your life in such a way to be of great service to many others. First and foremost, you must lay your own foundation and understanding before you can teach others. We will proceed accordingly, step by step. Indeed, as I have indicated, you may ask questions and we will answer your questions. I will make commentary as we continue on this road together.

"I will leave you, my friends, and come again in hope that you are receptive and eager for this opportunity to be together, speak together, and forge this bond between us. There are many who communicate with those like us and spirits in your planes of existence. It is not well known or well understood. Yet indeed, we are here to help prove that this is possible. We will bring forth much needed information and knowledge for the benefit of humanity.

"The soul has its own mind, its own abilities. This is where we wish you, my dear friend, to awaken, coming to that place that will allow you a deeper understanding and experience of truth. We will help you to comport yourself to that place of truth, soul awakening, and joy. This comes with love, a great source of love that humanity has not been able to avail themselves. This is the love of God. For in this great love and great energy that permeates the universe, the fuel for the soul is given. It allows for awakening its faculties long dormant, yet capable of being expressed and known as this great energy — this love of God activates great inner change and transformation.

"I ask you, my friend, to ask God for this gift. Not once, but many times. It will come as often as you ask and build accordingly. It is a simple process, one that cannot be mistaken for anything else. Once you feel and know this energy, you will recognize it for what it is, and you will want more. You must avail yourself of this one great truth. It is the greatest truth in all the universe. It is what will allow you to understand many things, allowing us to come to you in the way that we are now.

"So I leave you with this, my friend, and I shall return. May you know love, deep and abiding within you, growing and changing you —that great elixir of life. I am Orion and my love for you is great, my dear friend."

Orion did not disappoint with his latest dissertation. Jeremy's excitement continued to grow as he heard his teacher's words proclaiming a need for further development and expression of his gifts. He didn't take too seriously Orion's call for him to write a book and teach others the truth of otherworldly existences. That seemed too far-fetched to him, but he was convinced that the journey he was on would certainly be rich beyond his expectations. He was now fully on board, believing that Orion was real and that there was no doubt of his origins. For now, it was safe to be in their little triad of communication and discovery with all eyes on him, focusing a great deal of attention toward teaching him about his newfound friend and all that this entailed. What will come next is anyone's guess, he thought. But what he was experiencing now is exhilarating and fun. For a man so quiet and reserved, this was a gift beyond price.

Chapter 15

STAYING THE COURSE

Jeremy reflected on how good he felt being with Orion and Sadie on their sacred journey together. What Orion was sharing with him was astounding. Everything was changing so fast it made his head spin. Old routines and approaches were being transformed in ways that he had never imagined just a few weeks ago. There was no turning back now, he thought as he continued on with his work around Sadie's house. After their lunch together, they eagerly settled in for another session. And so Orion came once again to educate and inspire them both in the workings of the universe.

"I am Orion. The world is in great need of guidance, need of healing, need of all things that will bring it to a place of harmony and balance. We come to help educate and bring truth to those of you upon the Earth. We do not come just for your amusement, even your personal education. We come for all peoples on the Earth, utilizing this small beachhead of open-mindedness to assist those of you who desire to know more. We are here to help uplift and bring you to that place of understanding and truth.

"You are curious about our world and how we live. We will continue to educate you on this matter, though how we live and how we thrive on our planet is a secondary issue. Most importantly, we wish to support you on how you can change in order to live more harmoniously on your planet. That is a more pressing issue at this time since your planet is in a state of deep degradation and need.

"We wish to provide you with answers needed for a good life — a life lived without pain and disharmony. How fortunate we have been because we knew harmony from the beginning. All who are sentient and possess a soul in our universe have a beginning. Indeed, as your scientists seem to convey, humanity evolved from very rudimentary beginnings and traveled up the chain of evolution to what they are today. This is a good theory because it reflects the evolutionary processes that can be observed on Earth at this time.

"Yet, a creature with a soul is of a different nature. We both possess bodies that reflect animalistic qualities and, these traits and qualities have been honed and refined through evolution. Conversely, the evolution of the material body was never the end goal. Rather, we have both come to something quite different and unique. The body that evolved suddenly became a sentient creature with a soul. This happened on our planet as it happened on yours at different times. This quality of mind/soul sentience emerged in an instant because with the possession of a soul, everything changed. The creature that we both were long ago became something different, imbued with capabilities that no other creature on either planet possessed. Through the possession of a soul we were able to commune with the divine in a conscious way. The reality of God became a palpable thing which led to another primary discovery. We had the capacity to receive quantities of God's essence, which is the highest form of love in the universe and to take this in so that our souls reflected the divine, allowing changes to occur that opened gifts and faculties dormant within the soul. Since you too, Jeremy, possess a soul, the possibility of its development is within your grasp. The most fundamental teaching that we can offer you revolves around receiving this essence in a cumulative way. It is the next step towards humanity's evolutionary process. Until now, many of you have been obsessed with material accomplishment, focusing on the abilities of the mind to invent and create in your world. You have come to know the mechanics of the material universe and manipulated the material world to your advantage. Unfortunately, you have created a great imbalance as a result of these human endeavors, bringing about unfortunate consequences for yourselves and the entire planet.

"The evolutionary process on our planet was a very different matter. All the creatures who possess a soul have the added gift of free will, and we chose to follow the desires of our soul rather than our material minds. We chose love from the divine over control and independence, nurturing our souls with the essence of God . The harmony and grace that reflects life on my planet began very early in our history. Our choice to follow a road that was in sync with the divine plan rather than to walk a road that was of the individual's designation and desire has been a wise one. It is our hope that humanity might now choose differently. We never veered from our original course, and we have continued on this course for countless numbers of years. This result has brought us unimaginable rewards and gifts that add to a life which is rich and full. We live in harmony. We live in paradise. We live with awareness of our own soul's potentials and awareness of the love that our Creator has for us. All of these benefits have given us much joy and happiness.

"The consciousness of love comes with our inception and continues with our eternal progress. There is no ending for our species, nor death. Yes, we transition from a material body in time to that of a spirit body, but our souls continue to grow in the great illumination of love. Your planet has endured the choice of a humanity that follows its own will and desires rather than that of God's will and desires. You live in a world that is difficult, full of disharmony and lack of love, because you do not honor love or God as we do. Through fear and the desire for self-empowerment, most have rejected God, thinking that God is a deceitful being that needs to control and manipulate humanity. This is an unfortunate attitude preventing you from knowing the vast benefits that the Creator can provide. There is no price to be paid, only goodness and joy come of such a relationship. It is sad indeed to see how humanity has cheated itself out of the possibility of creating harmony and peace between you if only you could let go of your vanity and fear.

"What we have accomplished came readily because of the journey we have taken, endowed with spiritual and soul mind integrated into one. Call it a super mind, one that has great capacities and abilities to manipulate and utilize material to facilitate our well-being. The manifestation of material items does not deplete or defile our planet. Would you not wish to live in a world such as ours? Sadly, you live in a world where you suffer the consequences of your defilement of the Earth and each other. Indeed, it is a difficult place to live. I have great empathy and compassion for your struggles. Yet, the time is here for you to understand that there is a way out of your dilemma. You can live as we live, utilizing the forces and be clear and cognizant of the truths of both the universe within and outside of yourself.

"This is our goal, to help you come to realize your own potential that is completely buried within your taciturn mindful condition. We wish to liberate you, helping you find a way toward enlightenment and soul awakening while understanding the potentials of the soul and the soul integrated with your material mind. It is a powerful force for good, light, and harmony — a soul that is filled with a love that is naturally occurring within it plus the added love of God which we seek to receive daily. The soul will be refined, cleansed, and liberated from this human condition through this process. Your dear friend who has full understanding of this process, will educate you on these matters. It is not an easy task, but the process is simple. It requires your effort in prayer, setting your soul's intention toward the Creator of all, who is not elusive but available to each and every one.

"The simple truths regarding your purpose and existence have been taught before upon your planet. The way has been shown at times through various teachers. In your present world, these things are often ignored and very much misunderstood. Rather than making your way toward spiritual enlightenment simple, humanity has adorned it with many ideas, principles, rules, regulations, and judgments, transforming the simple truth of the divine into the complicated truth of man. What a tragedy this has been. Yet, many beings of light continue to make great effort to help you understand the simple truths of the universe and some have found these truths and live by them. There are few, but our wish is that there will be many who will subscribe to the awakening of the soul. This will mark the beginning of a new phase of evolution for humanity once the foundation is set and truth is lived as a reflexive act of affirming life. What is coming soon will furnish a renewed opportunity to discover the wonders of the soul.

"You may think of me as some being intent on preaching religion with efforts to convert you to my religion. I assure you that I have no religion. I merely know the truth that is of the universe and the very foundation of that truth is love. This is not a religion. It is a fact. This is not a prescribed way that you must follow and study for a long time in order to reach a certain level of advancement and knowledge or become an acolyte of my teachings. No, it is a very different course indeed. It merely requires you to open yourself to God and find what that opening will bring. Is this not so difficult? Is this onerous? Are you being led down the garden path? No, I offer you jewels of wisdom, jewels beyond price, something that you will carry with you forever. Indeed, the clarity and simplicity of these jewels are remarkable.

"There are beings upon your planet who have realized this journey and have accomplished this, but they do not have a physical body. They live in what they call the Celestial spheres. They are as adamant as we are to help humanity rise above their own degraded condition and find their way upon the journey I am suggesting. They too come to your world to help educate, uplift and love. We are a part and parcel of a great effort to help change your world for the better, to help bring enlightenment to humanity in order to save you from self-destruction.

"The Divine Source has designated me to be your guide and your teacher. I am privileged to have this responsibility and this gift. I will do my utmost to help you, provided that you are able to do what you can to facilitate this journey of awakening to truth and light. We are bonded, you and I, my friend. It cannot be any other way. For how else can we truly understand each other but to be close, and I am close to you. I am with you not only in this time together that we share, but I am with you often. I make much effort to impress upon you the thoughts and ideas that will lead toward greater understanding and truth. My love for you is great and I am close because love allows closeness to be a reality. It gives the channel the means of connection and communication. It is the connection of love that allows us to be, and my ability to transport myself from one place to another by thought. Within that thought, you become the individual that I can home in and appear in close proximity.

"This ability is shared with all of us on our planet who are mature enough to develop it. This is not difficult for us though in your mind it might seem impossible. You truly do not know your mind and its capacities. You merely know what you experience in this human world. I will show you things that will astound you. I will share with you truths and aspects of our life that you will find extraordinary. Advancement is the protocol for all the universe, moving forward, developing, refining, and growing in love, light, and truth. Understanding the universe, understanding the mechanics of the universe, understanding your own self and the mechanics of your being, are the many things you may come to know.

"We will not pile upon you too much, as your mind cannot possibly comprehend what is so foreign to you now. But we will make progress and in time you will write down and publish a book about these experiences.

Our hope is that many will read this book and understand that there is more out there than they can possibly imagine. In order to understand that, we are here to intervene and assist you to integrate the reality that begins inside of you and expands outward into the universe so you may be liberated from the shackles of your ignorance and your stultified condition. To remain in this condition will not allow you to truly realize what potential you carry within you.

"Love is the key, my dear friend. It unlocks the secrets of the Universe. Do not doubt this but consider it as something more valuable than any lesson that you may learn from me or anyone. Love is the key and you must come to know this and experience it in a way that makes it real and palpable in your life. The love of God, the Creator of all is immense, and each time you ask for a drop, a portion of this love, you come closer to the divine and you come closer to your true self. When you truly understand and apply this truth to your life, it will enable you to understand more complex truths, more complex ways and means of living in harmony in your world.

"It cannot be just one who enters into this journey of truth. There must be many. For the collective power of many will turn the tide of human evolution, diverting its present trajectory toward oblivion. Giving you the ways and means of traveling upon a road in which all may thrive in harmony will take some time. Yet, there is little time as you come closer to that cliff, and like lemmings, you will fall and continue to be in harm's way to a possible death. This great tragedy cannot happen, and so we will make every effort as will many other forces, to help divert this tragedy and bring you to a place of joyful realization of humanity's hidden potential.

"It starts with love, my brother, and so I give you my love, I dedicate myself to your progress. I am your friend, Orion, and I will leave you now and come soon. My love for you is great. God's Love for you is greater. Be in that love. Bask in that love. Breathe in that love and this will mark the beginning of a great journey."

With this, Orion left as quickly as he came, Sadie giving a great sigh of release, allowing the embodiment of her spirit to take hold once again. Jeremy was excited by what Orion had to say. The dream of the truths of a universe yet to be revealed was a staggering thought to him. He could not possibly have imagined the depth of Orion's knowledge and spiritual attainment. He was like an infant having a glimpse at complex mathematics. He didn't yet know the language or understand the context in order to appreciate such deep thoughts and perceptions but he was encouraged by Orion's message telling him that he would teach Jeremy what he could. He wondered whether he was up for the task, but the mere reality of Orion's presence in Jeremy's life was enough to spur him on.

Sadie suggested that they call it a day, as this day marked another milestone in their shared endeavors. It was best that Jeremy savor and contemplate what had happened rather than spend time in discussion, as that would come later, she thought. Now she needed to rest and Jeremy needed some time alone. So they parted ways until their next visit, Jeremy full of questions, but still unsure of how to ask and Sadie satisfied that they had made progress.

Chapter 16

SPIRITUAL TRUTH AND BEGINNINGS

Sadie and Jeremy's days returned to their normal routines. But Jeremy's mornings now began in prayer, focusing on receiving the *gift* Orion had described in their last conversation. His experiences were very subtle in the beginning — a mild burning sensation in his solar plexus. Before long, a sense of joy welled up inside of him, and he felt that he was being enveloped by a cloak of light.

"I'll be damned," he thought with a bit of astonishment. "This thing is real." He was now beginning to see the bigger picture — one that he could not have imagined just a few months ago. He was glad that he stumbled upon what Orion described as the highest truth in the universe. He could indeed see that God had guided him to Sadie and his encounter with Orion. A life that had been mundane and unexciting had transformed into a whirlwind of extraordinary experiences and insights. He sang God's praises as he worked and brought this newfound joy into everything. He didn't feel like the typical Christian restricted by theology and order. His was a reflection of pure joy welling up from his heart, unprovoked, and effusive. He was experiencing true happiness for the first time in his life. He knew with certainty that God had set him on a path of spiritual discovery and he was well on his way.

Every Tuesday was the highlight of their week as Jeremy and Sadie eagerly anticipated their next session with Orion. All other parts of their life did not compare to the vibrancy of their moments with Orion. His presence and depth of love for them drew them in like a moth to the flame, and they were willing to commune with him without any reservations.

Their routines were beginning to solidify. Jeremy would arrive a few hours early in order to accomplish whatever tasks Sadie had assigned to him. He happily complied as he felt he was getting the better half of the bargain, by far. Sadie would attend to her correspondence as Jeremy worked outside, weeding, cultivating, and pruning her garden. Sadie's house was a wreck, at best a teardown, but she was careful not to burden Jeremy with too much home repair as it would require far more time than their two-hour slot each week. Jeremy took charge in a way that ensured that Sadie was warm and safe in her little vine-covered cottage. Leaks in the roof were immediately attended to, rotten fence posts, and neglected corners of her ancient home were made fresh and watertight. Paint, spit, and polish eventually showed its results as her home began to take on an aura of respectability, a battle that Sadie gave up long ago.

Jeremy often felt energized as he worked around the property. It is as if some unseen force was ensuring that whatever he did in a physical way was blessed with a sense of mental clarity and capable body. He had never enjoyed his work as much as restoring Sadie's home to its original charm. Sadie appreciated everything he did. It was like God was ensuring that her home would be upheld and healed from years of neglect. She marveled at Jeremy's versatility and talent for solving what in her mind were insurmountable problems. The good Lord doth provide is all she could think as she saw Jeremy work and she prayed that he would be replenished and repaired in the process. She knew that everyone was blessed when service was performed with divine intent.

Sadie was a good cook. Her knowledge of herbs and spices ensured that her culinary creations were tasty and nutritious. Part of their arrangement included her special lunches, usually consisting of a hearty soup and homemade bread. She often would make a pie for dessert, using fruit or berries when in season. Today was cherry, Jeremy's favorite. Jeremy looked forward to her pies with the leftovers going into his lunch bag for the rest of the week.

When it was time for the session to begin, they sat in their respective chairs, ignoring plaintive cats and hair-lined throws intended to hide her worn furniture. The session began as it usually did with divine invocations followed by silence. Orion came as always with an onrush of energy and love.

"Thank you for your consistency and eagerness to engage in our communications together. I am pleased to see how you have taken to nurturing your soul with the spiritual light of God's essence, Jeremy. Do you have any questions for me today my friend?"

"Yes, I have many questions, but today I want to know more about your planet. Can you give us any technical details regarding the situation, size, and composition of your planet? And does it have a name," asked Jeremy with great deference?"

"I was wondering when you would ask me about these details, as the curiosity of humans is insatiable, answered Orion in his usual baritone voice. These technical matters are not so crucial for our lessons, but I will endeavor to supply the information you are seeking.

"Our planet is situated three spiral arms from your present position in the Milky Way galaxy. I have asked you to call me Orion because we are located in line of sight of this direction, although no means that you possess could pinpoint our location with any accuracy because the distance is too great. We are also closer to the central star cluster of our shared galaxy than Earth is. We inhabit a solar system that possesses a binary star system in which our planet revolves around, creating a similar solar cycle as your own. I don't believe I need to go into the technical details about the interaction of celestial bodies in the cosmos since this information is easily accessible by studying the laws of physics, as these laws are consistent throughout the universe.

"Our planet is somewhat larger than yours, situated in what is referred to as the Goldilocks Zone, not too far or too close to our suns. Our suns consist of one red dwarf and one class B star. One revolution of our planet around these stars requires a somewhat longer period of traversing than

Earth does. Our days are also longer; so the way we count time is different from yours.

"It would be difficult for you to pronounce the name that we call our Earth. The phonetic spelling is Eefonthriniti. This is as close as I can come to spelling it as our pronunciations are different from yours and our forms of communication involve psychic, emotional, and visual cues combined with a form of soul communication that creates a layered transference of information. This form of sharing would be overwhelming to your linear brains and present faculties. When we refer to our planet, many other descriptions and visual cues are integrated into the communication. Sharing a simple word describing our planet does a great disservice to what is understood as our home. My challenge in communicating with humans is to simplify my thoughts and concepts in order that you comprehend my meaning. Our language and ways of communication are so different from yours that I must share through this channel in a way that I might talk to a baby —simple, slow, and direct.

"You understand the makeup of the universe through chemical components that you describe as the Periodic Table. The chemical components of your planet are similar to ours, but we have more argon and selenium in our atmosphere and crust. When I took you both to our planet a while back, in thought only, you noticed a stark difference in colors. The sky and coloring of our vegetation was strangely different from yours. Your colorations are the result of substantial levels of oxygen in your atmosphere combined with the quality of light and intensity of your sun. Our capacity to breathe in this atmosphere is reflected in our physiology which processes air somewhat differently than you do on Earth. Abundant oxygen has a corrosive quality and although it exists on our planet, it is not as present as it is on Earth. The process of aging is greatly slowed partly because of the chemical makeup of our atmosphere. This is but one aspect of an environment that is conducive to longevity and good health. We are not engaged in physical nourishment as a form of pleasure, something that is so important to you on Earth. The focus of our lives reflects a desire for spiritual growth and awakening as well as creative endeavors which bring much pleasure. All things that bring a harmonious life for us are directly connected to our capacity to love.

"To love one another, to love our world, and to love our Creator is forefront in our desires and intentions. This is a very different outlook to what is the predominant culture and perspective on your planet — a planet based on fear and consumption in so many forms. Thus, we are here today Jeremy in what is merely another attempt to reach humanity. Our hope is that through these endeavors, some light will be shed on the true purpose of life and how you, as a species, may utilize wisdom shared by us and others to restore balance and harmony in your world and with you personally.

"I believe that we should close our session for today, Jeremy. We have shared a good deal of information for you to digest. I will say goodbye for now until our next appointed hour. With the blessings of our Creator, may you walk in peace and know the power of love to transform and heal."

Jeremy thanked Orion for answering his questions and adding some details.

Sadie's breathing began to change from a slow rhythm to a snort and deep intake of breath. Her eyes opened slowly as if waking from a deep sleep. Both she and Jeremy were enveloped in a blanket of peace which Orion brought with him as he engaged in his lessons. Another significant piece of the puzzle was added to Jeremy's understanding of why this connection was so important. A feeling of both hope and hopelessness overwhelmed him as he came to the conclusion that humanity is in deep trouble and that some of the responsibility for helping his fellow man out of the quagmire of this situation rests on his shoulders. The knowledge of Orion's home, and a better sense of it stood in sharp contrast to reality on Earth. Trying to reconcile the two gave Jeremy a headache. They were so far apart, not only in distance but in every aspect.

For now, he didn't want to engage with Sadie, who for the most part was oblivious to Orion's message. He wanted to go home and rest, contemplating the immensity of what lay ahead. So, he and Sadie said their goodbyes, confirming their next meeting.

Chapter 17

Jeremy and Sadie's Tuesday sessions continued to bring many answers as they remained open to Orion's purpose for them. Though they both continued to speculate and ruminate on the end goal that Orion had for this endeavor, they eagerly sat down to hear more of his extraordinary story. And so another session began, but this time without any prepared questions from Jeremy, instead with Orion initiating a dialogue consisting of what seemed a prepared lesson. Sadie willingly played her part as Jeremy fiddled with his tape recorder. He had taped most of their sessions and transcribed the words with both an electronic and paper version so he and Sadie could review what Orion said.

"Very well, it is Orion. I come once again to be with you and to speak to you, my beloved friends. I come to speak of things pertaining to your own personal growth and development. My intent is to awaken you to the tremendous power of love, a force that will help you to understand the deeper aspects of the universe. It is critical that you come to know how the universe operates and your place within it.

"In your world, many look to what is around them in order to give purpose and meaning to their lives. They seek multiple experiences and connections, filling their minds with information. This happens throughout their lives from childhood on, having learned many things through various interactions while accumulating material pleasures. The impetus to glean life's meaning and purpose through outside forces and experiences has created a very stilted view of the universe. To the vast majority, it is imperative to their deep understanding to bring critical and significant answers to the questions of life and its purpose other than what is derived from external forces.

"Yet, humanity continues to empower the outer world to manifest their own mindful inclinations and ambitions. It is very difficult to penetrate beyond the mental condition that this imposed reality has created. Thus, humanity continues to congregate together in thought and action toward surface gratification and material expressions. Our world is very different from yours. From a child's conception, their parents pour love upon them. The love is not only the source of the parents' innate abilities to love, they also become conduits and channels for universal love pouring toward the newborn soul. Therefore, that child has a great start, a wondrous capacity, and openness that is inherently a part of them because their souls have been sensitized to love, nurtured by love, and awakened by love. The emotional, physical, and spiritual capacities of a child born on my planet are far greater than those on your planet. There is great joy within the child, no pain, no stress, and no situations that create fear or anguish. Rather, all is love and light — an ideal world that I know you aspire toward. The difference is that your people continue to look outward to find solutions and self-expression as an external source rather than looking within, nurturing that place which is the soul.

"In the core of every human being is a soul and that soul has a dynamic expression, the source of all life animated, of motivation, of thought, and perception. In your world, you see this as the mind, a material mind in all its machinations and expressions. In my world, the mind is centered within the soul. The soul can grow and expand in consciousness from birth onwards as abilities and capacities of the soul are greatly enhanced as each child is taught how to access the great source of love, that energy that is a reflection and expression of God. There is only one crucial outward connection that is necessary and that is cultivating the relationship between the individual soul and the soul of God, the two essences combining and relating as the individual receives this great gift of the palpable essence of God's love.

"A solid foundation built by love is set from the beginning and expands, fostering a harmonious life. It is a life that knows no suffering, no pain, but merely joy and continuous awakening, gleaning the knowledge of the universe through the perceptions and consciousness of the soul. Developments such as this allow us to travel between our planet and yours, and between our planet and many others. It allows us a leisurely but productive life. Our endeavors, our focus, our ambitions are very different from yours. We have no need to put a great deal of effort into creating material objects and working toward material gain. Our needs are simple, and they are met in simple ways. We are able to manifest structures, food, and any object that our bodies require. We do possess technologies that enhance our spiritual and material bodies, helping us to integrate aspects of soul consciousness. Our lives are simple in some ways, and very complex in others. That which motivates us in the material sense has been so simplified that it has become a very minor part of our existence. It is the honing of consciousness, the expression of love emanating, surrounding, and connecting with others and the universe that motivates us in our endeavors. It becomes the great nurturer as we receive from the source of all. We express this abundance, this gift of love in everything that we do, and everything that we are. A child is not only nurtured and loved by his or her parents, but also nurtured by all that they encounter in their lives.

"There is great creativity on our planet. The arts are highly refined. The capacity to create beautiful homes and edifices for gatherings are expressed collectively. Yet, even these needs are not as great because our population is stable and modest in numbers. Our structures and societies have been long-standing for millennia. Our planet, the ecosystem, the planetary structures that are an inherent part of it do not suffer by our presence, but are enhanced by the expressions and capacities we have to manifest those things that are of benefit to our world.

"We have much wisdom and knowledge as to how to go about our lives in a way that does not detract or damage the natural order of our planet.

Yes, with our presence upon our Earth, there is always some impact; but because of our capacities for healing, and expressions of light and love, we are able to mitigate this damage to the point where nothing is truly lost or depleted.

"You worry about your Earth being self-sustaining, yet the source of that capacity is not well understood. We have much to teach you, and much to give to you if you are willing to open yourself to these things.

"Though the Earth continues to be self-sustaining, that capacity is diminishing daily and we have great concern for the health of your planet and its capacity to continue to sustain life through the rhythms and cycles that it inherently possesses. It would take many hundreds of years for you to change your ways, implementing that knowledge and understanding of both spiritual and material in order for the Earth to be as our planet is. But it is possible. Our goal is to help humanity in this process. It first begins with our initial contact. But this is only a very minor beginning of a very long and intricate process of healing and discovering the truth. You cannot assume that you know everything, and that your perceptions of the world are correct. In fact, you know very little, and your perception of the world is for the most part incorrect. You are unable to see the intricacies, the beauty, the energy, the interactions, the ebb and flow of natural cycles, and systems that bring a depth of empathy and understanding of them. Rather, you see from a superficial perspective, through your five senses, and your mindful integration of information as bits and pieces of data continue to be infused into your mind.

"Yet, such perceptions are only the tip of the iceberg in terms of what is truly happening in your world and in the Universe as a whole. The Universe is multi-layered — a reality that is reflected in the infinity of possibilities. You have inklings of your own body and the intricacies of that body. You understand that many cells work together and that there is something mystical that allows these cells to communicate in such a way as to sustain your body. Many do not understand that they have an energy body, or spirit body that contributes to sustaining the cellular body. The Chinese call it chi, but this too provides a somewhat inadequate explanation of the entire system of both physical and spiritual relationships inherent in the body. The interplay between these two aspects within you is crucial and powerful. When you understand these two components more thoroughly and deeply, you will come to know the source of illness, great pain, and suffering in the body. You will be able to heal these things without the course interventions used today.

"Yes, the mind does play its part, but your reality goes much deeper than this. It is the health and well-being of the spirit that is important. The health and well-being of the spirit is determined by the health and well-being of the soul. Essentially, there are three levels of consciousness within you — the soul, the spirit, and the body. How much do you understand soul? What credence do you give soul? It is a well-used word in your world, but is it truly understood? Many believe that the soul is an amorphous thing that is referred to by religious institutions. There is often a desire to withdraw from such principles because of the actions and reputations that many churches have created over the course of their history; this brings negative reactions and resistance to truths that are in part understood by these religions.

"Your soul is not acknowledged by many in your secular world. It is something best forgotten and ignored. This is the great tragedy of your species. Those who seek soul tend to adorn it with so many layers of projected thought and paradigms that you are burdened by these complexities. The soul, in essence, needs freedom to be expressed. The consciousness of the soul, and simplicity of true intuitive understanding of its being and presence within is nothing like that of the mind. That is a great blessing indeed!

"There is much work to do in your world in order to clear away the heaviness of erroneous human thought to bring in true consciousness that begins with the soul. The soul may rise up through the layers to your conscious awareness and material existence if allowed to do so. My friend, it is difficult for us to see the suffering that you have on your planet. It is difficult to see the choices that you have made, and are making daily. Liken us to a parent who is wise and understands many things, yet sees their child make poor decisions over and over again!

"We have great compassion for you and great love. We wonder why so many onerous and difficult decisions have been made to bring about such great disharmony and suffering. Why is this? You know the mechanics and understand the law of free will, your capacity to act on your own volition. Yet, we wonder why you lack wisdom, though wisdom exists within you. It is within the soul. Even your spirit and body have a measure of wisdom. You continue to ignore these things, and dance to the music of materialism and all that this entails. The constructs of human thought and deed are reshaped over and over again, expressed and invented as you continue to mine the resources of your world and transform them into material means that are not necessarily needed but desired. Is this what brings meaning to your life? To make more and more material objects, to surround yourself with more material comforts, to seek out one another in an orgy of materialism, a life shallow and vain in an ever sought-after retreat from the possibility of pain, even death?

"This is not being true to your creation, as you are much more than this. You have much more to give to one another. You have much more to express in your material world in such a way that there can be greater harmony. Much can be given and understood, but you must make the effort to go within, to nurture love within you, to bring the great divine love, that source of all love into yourself. In this way you may be transformed, resurrected from the dormancy of a soul neglected to one that is alive, vital, and filled with life and love.

"There are many solutions to your dilemmas that exist and the capacity to understand them exists. Your ambitions and goals must change radically in order to be receptive to these solutions. You will not lose yourself with this shift of perspective, but the unique person that you are will be enhanced by the soul awakened to its gifts. The capacities within that soul can be realized so that you may understand the magnificence of your own creation, your own being, and join with us in the Universe as equal partners — equals in a universe that is populated by many, many souls eager for continued connection, interaction, and expression. This can be accomplished in so many ways that you could not possibly imagine at this time; but they will come to the fore provided the future that is offered is accepted.

"I will not speak more today, but I thank you for listening to me and allowing me to express my thoughts to you, so to help lighten and brighten, giving to humanity hope for a new world — a future that is promising and beautiful. Blessings to you, my friends! I am Orion, and I love each of you, my beautiful friends of Earth. God bless you in love.

His message was both intriguing and frightening, hinting tough times ahead — but also hopeful for the future. Jeremy was beginning to understand the seriousness of the situation, and how Orion and others were intent on assisting humanity in what will be a very changed world. Jeremy certainly felt that the world was changing, and not for the better. Living in a small town lacking in the frenetic rush of big city life, he felt cocooned in his little bit of heaven; yet all that was about to change if Orion's predictions were to be taken seriously. It was so much to contemplate and consider as he bid his goodbyes to Sadie who still seemed a bit 'out there'.

She seemed to be going deeper into a trance state as they progressed with their communications and this created within her a sense of detachment as her consciousness was fogged by the afterglow of Orion's presence. She was glad that Jeremy took his leave quite quickly.

She needed time to rest. Not just from the rigors of their time together, but because of the effects of her physical condition, fighting off the cancer which was progressing quite rapidly. She found out the news only recently, as she was not feeling her old self and decided to make a rare visit to her doctor. She knew that something was not right, but she was surprised by the diagnosis. The doctor was grim with his prognosis and insisted that she undergo the harsh treatments that came with the disease. She would have nothing of it. If it was her time to go; she was more than ready to be released from this harsh world. The doctor was flabbergasted. He argued with her, and described what would happen without the treatments. She would have nothing of it and stormed out of his office. He merely shook his head in disbelief muttering something about her eccentric ways.

She began to wonder if there was enough time to complete her task with Jeremy and Orion. Though she knew that she had very little control in the matter, she hoped that God would grant her the time to finish what was started.

Chapter 18

MORE REVEALED

From all outward appearances, the world seemed its old self — spinning on its axis, providing the impetus for continued human endeavor and industry. Jeremy wondered when that would all change and new ways of living would usurp the old. He was less inclined to share the information that Orion had given with those around him, so he assumed his usual casual demeanor, much to the relief of many. It seemed that he wasn't as unstable as some had thought, responding to some of the radical changes observed in his recent behavior. Old Jeremy was back, more precisely, he was more grounded and clearer in his demeanor. His initial blush of enthusiasm and bravado quickly turned into a more circumspect approach. This was partly because of a conversation he recently had with Sadie who warned him that the more he acted oddly toward the outside world, the more trouble he would make for himself. Sadie spoke from experience since she was still unable to change the attitudes of many around her who judged her as a crazy witch. She asked him if he would like to follow in her footsteps as the town's most eccentric person? That shocked him, and he realized that the price would be too great to declare his newfound beliefs with the town folks. After all, he was communicating with not only aliens, but with God himself. Common sense dictated that he make accommodations with those who were part of his normal life. After all, he had a business to run and a life outside of what was happening with him and Sadie. And so he lived a dual life, one exciting and full of surprises while the other was mundane and familiar. He was grateful for the former and in a way, for the roundedness of the latter.

His next session with Sadie did not disappoint as they evoked Orion's presence once more. Orien introduced himself and continued from where he left off the last time they met.

"It is Orion, shall we continue with our dissertations? Today, I wish to speak about the social and political conditions of my planet, contrasting with yours. As I have indicated, we live in a harmonious environment, one that considers all and does not leave any individual out. There are none who are deprived, ill, or lack sustenance and shelter, those basic requirements for every soul to live on the material plane. For the most part, our thinking reflects the needs of the collective rather than the needs of the individual. We have very few institutions, for we have no need for them. Schooling is done at home. Shared responsibilities between family members and extended family members who belong to the collective community ensure that there is adequate teaching and demonstration of knowledge for the young. Much experience is gained within the family unit as well as interacting with other individuals, families, and elders while demonstrating various abilities and gifts taught to our children through the group collective. This way of living was common in your past but was far less refined than our present ways.

"Our children stay with their parents for a much longer period of time than yours. Since our lifespan is in the hundreds of years, children within the family unit continue to stay together for what could be as long as one hundred years. Hence, the progression of life is slower in some ways than yours. We are not in a great hurry to become adults. Yet, the maturation of a child is similar to yours, up to twenty years to attain physical maturity. Of course, there are always exceptions, and a child may leave at any time from the family unit. Since love and respect are a mainstay of family unity, there is less impetus to leave. Indeed, the desire to form couples, mate together, and create a family of their own is as strong in our society as in yours. However, the need to establish a permanent bond with another is not as great. Liaisons and relationships flow naturally between the sexes, even when they are living with their family of origin. There are no hard and fast rules in our society regarding the establishment of families. Rather, where love springs forth, it is acceptable to be together in whatever form this may take. Relationships between those of the same sex are quite acceptable and fluid. There is no judgment or expectations in the ways that the individual may contribute to society.

"Our economies are so very different from yours. Although there is very little government, there are collectives centered around communities that ensure that individual needs are taken care of. When I say that individuals are cared for, I do not mean that we are in great need or have physical or mental impediments. This does not exist. Rather, interaction between communities and members of communities is common and frequent. Within these communities or collectives, there exists a great generosity where everything is shared among many individuals. It is quite common for individuals from other collectives to form relationships outside of their communities, ensuring genetic diversity and providing a variety in perspective and approach to life, thereby forming well bonded and healthy families.

"The bond is an agreement between individuals in a relationship that is not considered permanent, but may last for many hundreds of years. Commonly, relationships change and evolve. The spiritual/ physical attraction of one individual toward another motivates different relationships and commitments. Of course, when a family is created and children are born, there is an understanding that the family will stick together and continue to nurture one another for a considerable period of time. Like all things, there is a beginning and an ending of the formulation and dissolution of families. This is not a hardship. Nor is anyone alone, nor are they lonely. Yet, each individual chooses the trajectory of their life for a certain period and may choose to live alone for some time and engage in a relationship at another time. Deep respect flows between every individual toward all others, developing lifelong bonds that are complex and varied. Such bonds may last for a lifetime or a day, but the depth of love displayed is deeper than anything you experience on your planet. The closest you may come to it is to consider the love a mother has for her children, yet we love strangers more than you love your kin.

"Each individual's capacity to love all other individuals is demonstrated by the development of the love principle within them. They are a soul infused with the essence of love that flows from the Divine source, and their ability to express love is great indeed. Upon meeting such individuals in the flesh, you would find the experience of connecting with their beautiful soul quite overwhelming. It is an attraction that you would find magnetic in nature and highly desirable. Although we are slightly different in our appearance to those of you on Earth, I believe that you would not find us unattractive. You might even perceive us to be a living God or a prophet, yet we are neither. We are merely an expression of the potential of our souls manifested by the unique qualities that they possess. Your experience with me is a reflection of a very restricted expression of who I am in order to facilitate this communication. Otherwise, both of you would find my presence very uncomfortable since neither of you possesses the soul development that I do. I am not saying this to intimidate or criticize either of you. I am sharing with you the reality of the situation between us. I come into your presence in such a way that is comfortable for all concerned. It's an expression of love, not superiority, since I honor you as my brother and sister as I do all of humanity.

"Our governing bodies are designed to serve and do so with no self-interest in this service, rather, a desire to support and bring harmony among all groups on our planet. There are no individual countries, per se — although, like your own world, there are differences in appearance and some cultural variations, but not as varied as your planet. Homogenization of the races is quite evident throughout our planet due to inter-marrying and the way in which our societies function. But this happened eons ago. Therefore, the distinctions indicate some variations of skin color depending upon their geographic location. It is similar to your own planet where there are northern habitations and southern habitations, and tropical climates and cooler climates. Therefore, some differences have evolved.

"Every individual can move freely upon our planet. There are no restrictions that limit us in travel or movement. Our population is not as great as yours. Your world is greatly burdened by population, where ours is not. There is a commonsense approach to forming families and contributing to our overall population. Each one has a sense of when they may procreate. Most commonly, the nuclear family is small, consisting of two children and two parents. Families may also live with other families collectively in one habitation. Often, there is an extended family of grandparents, great-grandparents, and those who cohabitate but are not blood relatives. As I mentioned before, individuals live for an extended period of time so the possibility of blending together many members within a family is great. Consequently, their homes and places of habitation may be quite large with many rooms and many places to repose and socialize.

"We create such habitations by utilizing our ability to reform materials of our planet at will into beautiful spaces in which to live. There is no need for factories as you have in your world. Objects are created mentally using innate metaphysical attributes in order to reform natural materials into what is required. We do not kill animals so that we may eat. Primarily, we eat vegetables and fruits, drink pure water which we create with a variety of naturally flavored beverages. Animals are our friends. There is not the variation of animals upon our planet as yours, but there is no predation on our planet either. Harmony prevails in this situation as animals live together in harmony, and live with us in harmony. Yes, we have pets, those animals that prefer to be with us, and we communicate psychically together. Indeed, we have conversations, and we have interactions with those creatures that are well suited for domestication. The animals' minds are easily accessed and communicated with whether they are domesticated or wild.

"Our entertainment is varied indeed. We have festivals, and we encourage creativity in the arts. We have music. We have plays which reflect elaborate pageantry, even a sort of video, but it is different from yours. One individual projects the story holographically in great detail. These individuals are highly talented and imaginative, and there is often a component of learning that is incorporated into the story. Children are very drawn to these forms of entertainment and learning. They also play together as they do on your planet.

"Our forms of transportation are by thought. We are able to materialize and dematerialize ourselves at will, as well as transport material objects in the same way. At times we utilize vehicles that run by thought, transporting people as well as various items. We also trade with other planets various resources, minerals, even food commodities that are highly prized. Each planet has an excess of something that they are willing to share with others, and so the sharing happens amongst many planets that are highly evolved and sophisticated like our own.

"We do not have a currency like you do in order to pay for goods. We share what we have with others and others share what they have with us. There is no sense of obligation or debt toward individuals or even other planets. Our sense and desire to share is a reflection of our love for one another and for those who inhabit distant worlds. Harmony ensues because there is no great need for material gain, as our needs are well met regardless. Our needs are filled harmoniously, generously, and often. The stress and competitive culture that is so much a part of your world is eliminated because we have enough and know how to obtain things using knowledge and abilities centered on the love principle and our innate generosity towards one another.

"At some point you will come to understand how this is accomplished. We are enthusiastic and willing to help you come to this once your frame of mind and ability to accept a new way of being on your planet is realized. At this juncture, you are not capable of stepping forward in this way, releasing the burdens and disharmony that you possess and express to one another. But know this, the time of great change for you is coming and it will be swift in comparison with other evolutionary processes that humanity has encountered. But first you must come to a breaking point where your systems, and your way of life no longer function adequately, no doubt creating within you great fear and great need. Our hope is that humanity will be receptive to our interventions which, in many ways, reflect divine intervention. You cannot go on living the way you do, feeding off of one another and carrying such great burdens and unhappiness because your needs are not met. It is a reflection of your ignorance and misunderstanding of what life is. You do not understand the power of love to create harmony together on your planet. This is the one great lesson that must be learned. Love must replace fear. Love must be in everything that you are, and everything that you do.

"Yes, you are a long way from this state of love. Although your society feels love toward families, mates, and children, the love you feel is meager compared to the love that I am referring to. It is a love that emanates from the soul. The capacity for the soul to love has the potential to be infinite if the individual can access love from the Divine source. Everything that we do upon our planet reflects love and is love. The way our societies are organized, share, and communicate with one another is a reflection of love — love that is deep and abiding. It is a love that grows because we seek the nurturance of our souls by receiving what your dear friend calls divine love. It is the essence of the universe that is infused with this Divine energy. It is something that can be obtained by desire — asking for it in simple prayer and connection with the Divine source. It is the one great truth that unifies all people wherever they may be.

"We have great centers in each community where we come together to pray and commune with the creator of all. I would not call this a religion as you see religions, but rather a function of our society's desire to participate in joyful gatherings that reflect a need to be with God. In this way, each is nurtured. Each receives more of the great universal love through our collective prayers as well as individual efforts in prayer. Each expands in light and love, and in abilities and gifts. When they mature, they will have a greater capacity to contribute to society with their gifts, enhancing our lives together and sharing gifts that reflect the soul's intrinsic qualities and abilities.

"Humanity sees itself as possessing a mind and material brain as the great gift — as the solution to all your problems, where you merely need to apply your mental capacities to solve them. Indeed, you have created interesting and complex inventions as a result. Yet, I say to you that the greatest capacity for creativity, understanding, invention, and application that is harmonious with everything upon your planet does not come from the mind. It comes from the mind of the soul — a soul that is well-developed by Divine source. This is what we wish to teach you.

"We are not the only ones who are poised to help humanity. You have upon your planet higher spheres of existence, where individuals who have lived their short life on Earth, have progressed through various spheres of consciousness toward very high and beautiful places which you call heaven. We work with these individuals, collaborating with them. They are the initiators of a far-reaching plan to reshape human consciousness into something more harmonious and sustainable.

"It is not too late to save your planet from annihilation; but the systems, flow, and rhythms of your planet in its natural form are being burdened by your activities and a lack of respect and love for it. You continue to take so much from it, returning nothing that will support and maintain its equilibrium. There is great concern among us regarding the condition of your planet as it continues to show signs of stress and disharmony. It is coming to a crisis point and will be quite destructive toward all that humanity has built. Your Earth has its own consciousness, and each planet has its own consciousness. As a result, your Earth is fighting you, and it conflicts with you as you are in conflict with it.

There are changes within your climate and natural systems that are causing great havoc amongst humanity. Unfortunately, it will only worsen because the planet is determined, having the capacity to change Earth conditions to such a degree that humanity will not be capable of living in the way that it does. Your inventions and systems will fail. Your way of living will become obsolete and in many ways, there will be a reset regarding how humanity will thrive in your world.

"This reset is coming soon, my friends. We and others are making a great effort to communicate with you and to establish our presence with those of you who are sensitive and receptive enough to know us. We do so out of love and concern — out of a desire to help you regain your equilibrium, and for Earth to regain its natural balance to be healthy and vital once again. As the Earth changes and reflects greater light and harmony, humanity might flourish and know a good life. It won't be one of deprivation, fear, anger, and lack of love, but one of love, grace, beauty, and harmony. This is our goal. This is the goal of many others who continue to gather around you in this world. It is a goal to help nurture something that is more in harmony with the laws of creation — laws we all must live by that ensure balance and harmony in the universe.

"I will continue to share more details about myself and my planet and our endeavors together. We will carry on with these communications in hope that you will share them with others. Yes, we are sounding the alarm, and yet we are bringing hope. It is because the great Creator of all has compassion and love for you on Earth, and ensures that those who suffer will find a way out of their suffering. It will be the ones who are in disarray and disharmony that will find a way toward harmony and peace. And, those who lack love or feel unloved will find a way toward love. These simple truths are vital for the functioning of the universe. We will continue to teach these things to you, Jeremy, and you will find yourself in the fortuitous situation of teaching others.

"I will leave you now, my friends, and come again soon. I love you both and care for you deeply. I will continue to uphold you. May light shine upon you and may you come to know your own soul and its abilities and capacities to love and express many things. May the blessings of the Creator be yours and the love of the Creator flow upon you and into you until you are transformed and awakened and in the light. Thank you. Thank you, all."

Jeremy was beginning to understand the sense of urgency that Orion was giving them both regarding this project. It seemed that there was little time before the world was about to change in unimaginable ways. If what Orion says is true, then anything else that may seem a priority in his life was irrelevant. No wonder their extraterrestrial friends are making such a concerted effort to make contact. According to them, historical events were imminent and could prove fatal to many on the planet. Humanity needed to wake up and the time to do so is short, according to Orion.

Chapter 19

GIVING OVER TO TRUTH

Jeremy felt a new tension as he took heed of Orion's message about the fate of the world. His gut told him that what Orion was saying rang true, but his dilemma was in how to apply this knowledge in real time. It was surely in conflict with the common perceptions of those around him. Jeremy would continue to walk the fine line between living his old life and contemplating what would be required of him and needed for our troubled world.

Jeremy's newfound truth had come with a double-edged sword that cut through the illusions of the human condition to the truth of the matter. Jeremy found himself once again on the roller coaster of inner conflict as he tried to discern the truth between his illusions and what was real. He wanted peace above all else, yet peace was as elusive as his desire for simplicity and happiness. The dark shadow of his dilemmas haunted him, causing great pain and turmoil. Yet, he managed to put on a brave face, comforted by the faithful friendship he shared with Sadie.

Sadie had a way about her that ensured a balanced and wise approach. She had lived long enough in this world to understand that she could not solve all its problems and it made no sense to ruminate over the darkness of the human condition. It could all quickly become overwhelming and out of control if one allowed it. One step at a time was always the best approach.

She knew that Jeremy was not handling Orion's news very well. It was obvious that Orion's dire warnings were bringing great grief to him. She coped by bringing her concerns to God knowing she had neither the ability or the opportunity to make things right in the world. After all, we all possessed the gift of free will. Therefore, the complexity of human action and thought was far too much for anyone to have a positive influence on. We were all going to hell, and there was little she could do about it, she thought. But it appeared that there was a plan which Orion was a part of, and that gave her a measure of comfort. Although she had no idea how this plan would be implemented, she had faith that the goodness of the universe would win over and dispel all that is bad. Why else would Orion say these things if there was indeed a way out of this mess, she thought.

All she and Jeremy could do was to continue to meet together and receive Orion's instructions. Engaging the brain too much in big picture speculations would only lead to confusion and heartache, she thought. She resolved to tell Jeremy as much before he became overwhelmed with concern and anxiety over the fate of the world. This would surely be a heavy burden for such a sensitive man.

Their next meeting began with her wise counsel, which had a calming effect on him. Jeremy wanted to push the conversation further. He wanted help in finding a way to be in the world while living with such a terrible secret that he wasn't able to share with others.

"The world is asleep Jeremy." remarked Sadie. "Until people wake up, there will be no viable solutions to remedy the human condition. What Orion is telling us is that we need to be patient and consistent with our own process of awakening before we can help anyone else," Sadie confided in her usual bluntness. "Our world is full of impatience and a desire for instant gratification. No one wants to put much effort into their own spiritual awakening when there is no material payoff," she lamented. "Most keep plugging along, hoping for future rewards, but typically, when realized, leave them with a hollow and dissatisfied feeling. The world is a mess, but must we continue down the road of lost souls, or forge ahead with our own pursuit of spiritual truth?" she said with utmost seriousness.

Jeremy knew that she was right. There were no perfect solutions without first finding his own way to enlightenment. So he began to decompress from the troubles that his mind had created. Both he and

Sadie settled in for yet another session without much of the mental noise that Jeremy had been engaging in since their last transmission.

Orion came quickly into the picture as Jeremy and Sadie had established a fixed routine which helped to facilitate his arrival.

"I am Orion. I come to continue with my dissertation for publication. My friend, Jeremy, in order to awaken the soul, you must have a heart that is full, coming into alignment with the soul. All souls in the universe have a heart. That heart has a physiological expression within the body but is also part of the emotional and spiritual expression of the individual. This has been referred to in many ways in your world and in ours. Poetry and songs have been written on the subject of the heart, an essential component of love. In many ways there is a physiological component to love that begins in the heart. I urge you my friend to have heart in your efforts in relation to spiritual growth and awakening. It will also give you a key to understanding your own nature and being.

"Many guard their hearts well, thus there is little feeling or understanding of their source. This great impediment has caused much suffering in your world. In mine, we are open with our hearts. To be spiritually healthy, it is important to be attuned to your own emotions, those feelings that lead to deeper spiritual insights and experiences. Since we do not verbally communicate, all is done telepathically. The emotions of the heart are a component of this form of communication. Without it, communication is dry and lacks depth. With feelings and expressions such as love, these communications are rich and full of meaning. This must be learned on your planet. An unguarded heart is an expression of strength, not weakness. One who is full of feeling is open to the Universe and the influence of divine forces. Where there is coldness and mindful calculation derived from intellect, there is a lack of connection and warmth between souls. Your world is full of such behavior, and it has caused much misunderstanding and pain.

"There is so much that humans must come to understand what exists and is suppressed within them. The beginning of spiritual awareness requires opening of the heart, and feeling the center of the individual. These centers are well expressed as chakras — concepts that define the energetic parts of the spirit body. Opening the heart chakra is an important component of spiritual awakening. I urge you to continue to be sensitive to these parts of yourself, and be sure of your feelings, thoughts, and all that is happening within your body, spirit, and soul. Awareness and awakening to spiritual awareness are multi-dimensional. You cannot awaken one thing and guard another. Many parts of you are connected like a string of pearls. When one part is nurtured, then it ignites those parts around it, and so on. It creates a chain reaction that can be quite powerful and intense, contributing to the deep development of what we call soul.

"Those who pursue a spiritual life often describe this as an awakening experience. It is to experience what is happening within the individual as the spiritual centers awaken. The great center of the individual is the soul which must awaken and is the foremost goal. Soul awakening, and many other small awakenings are ignited as well. In your world, many see them as the key to their spiritual progress and to some degree, they are.

"Unfortunately, many miss the significance of awakening the core of their being by nurturing the soul. Most often, they are engaged in metaphysical and intellectual development which bypasses the soul altogether. They don't recognize that a powerful aspect of the awakened soul is capable of orchestrating and bringing into focus an understanding of all aspects of being. I urge you to pray and seek diligently the great gift from the Divine. The essence of love from the soul of God will bring you to the consciousness of soul, thereby opening multiple doors of experience, insight, and perception.

"It is important to begin with the awakening of the soul. Then all other aspects will fall into place and the awakening will be a harmonious experience rather than one that is jarring and lacks coordination and harmony within you. There are many who force these openings, eager to find their way along a spiritual path, and they often become lost within the minutiae of their experience. They are unable to navigate a course to something more relevant and deeper. I encourage you on the path of soul awakening, a path that cannot be fulfilled without your dedication to forging a relationship with your Creator. It begins in this way and there is no ending to this journey. Every planet in the Universe needs to begin in this way if they are to truly progress beyond the limited perspective of the material mind and intellect. Understanding the nature of your duplicate self which is often called the 'spirit body,' only brings you halfway towards the realization of the true self, embodied primarily in soul. Without fostering spiritual awareness, the development of true soul perception and building a deep capacity for love, all other pursuits and universal misunderstandings will not bring humanity to greater enlightenment and harmony. Building a foundation of love is the only way forward for any race, no matter where they are within the Universe. Understanding the love principle is essential in human endeavor and progress. Without this understanding, little changes in the heart, even if much progress is made materially.

"You must begin with love, and to begin with love, you must know your own heart. Be true to this part of yourself. Do not underestimate the power of an open heart, seek with deep emotion, and feel the truth. I urge you to begin this way, without hesitation or doubt. What is often called faith is really a reflection of an open heart to God. Faith is a feeling and knowing that God is here to comfort, awaken, heal, and bring you to that place of great mystical awareness of His universe, presence, and love for all.

"You must seek this beyond all else Jeremy and do not hesitate. As you seek this new journey, the depth and breadth of our communication will be enhanced by your pursuits. You will find yourself able to know and understand things that within your mind are beyond reach. Yet, with your soul mind, it is easily grasped. There is much for you to do. There is much for all of us to do. The world is on the cusp of great transformation and change, and we must speed the process of your awakening so you are ready for what is to come. We will help you along this road, but we cannot do so without your receptivity and eagerness. Desire is the key to awakening. You must find your way beyond the constrictions of your mind and your feelings. Where fear is predominant, you must replace it with joy and openness. Where biases and judgment prevail, you must open yourself to acceptance and love. Free yourself, my brother, from old restrictions that are vestiges of mindful patterns derived from your earthly life. Be ready to accept a new way with divine forces guiding you forward. Your progress depends on it.

"Thank you for listening to me. I hope you will take my words to heart and seek out that which your heart desires, bringing it into your reality and consciousness. My love is with you all. Blessings are yours from the great source of all. I am Orion. Thank you."

The wisdom that Orion shared continued to arouse deep respect within Jeremy. He felt as if he was communicating with not just someone from another world, but also a beloved uncle who was both generous and kind. The bond that was developing between them was palpable, forged in love and truth. A form of truth that was beginning to make sense the more he heard from his trusted sage. Although they were not from the same planet, Jeremy was beginning to understand that the differences were not as great. Orion's term 'brother' was indeed appropriate. How different was Orion from those who inhabited the Earth? Though it was obvious that Orion's life experience was completely foreign to his own, he felt a kinship, a kind of human bond. Orion looked different, a sort of Gandalf figure compared to a Hobbit, yet the affection and respect shared between these two fantasy figures were similar to what Jeremy was experiencing with his improbable friend. You couldn't make this up he thought with a wry smile.

Sadie was beginning to awaken from her deep trance state. Jeremy knew to be still and quiet while she was coming to. Any loud noises or disturbances before, during or after these sessions would jar Sadie to the point of gaining consciousness too quickly and cause her some grief. Jeremy waited until she appeared awake.

Sadie was tired, more tired than she had ever been. The juggernaut of unchecked cancer cells within her was taking its toll. She was not afraid to die. In many ways she welcomed it because she had already seen the land which she was destined to inhabit, and it was most certainly a far better place than this harsh earth. Of course, she wanted to finish her work here, especially with dear Jeremy and Orion. This desire sustained her despite the discomfort and pain which was at times acute. She did not let on to Jeremy what was going on in her body. She felt that it would just add to the burdens that he was already carrying — best to be quiet and keep the status quo, she concluded.

She wanted to go to her bed and sleep off the weight of her present condition. She felt drugged by it and knew that her spirit and stellar friends were doing their best to uphold her. She asked with insistence for Jeremy to help her to her bed, explaining that she wasn't feeling well. Jeremy kindly led her to her bed and left to resume the other chores that were waiting for him.

"Thank you for listening to me. I hope you will take my words to heart and seek out that which your heart desires, bringing it into your reality and consciousness. My love is with you all. Blessings are yours from the great source of all. I am Orion. Thank you."

The wisdom that Orion shared continued to arouse deep respect within Jeremy. He felt as if he was communicating with not just someone from another world, but also a beloved uncle who was both generous and kind. The bond that was developing between them was palpable, forged in love and truth. A form of truth that was beginning to make sense the more he heard from his trusted sage. Although they were not from the same planet, Jeremy was beginning to understand that the differences were not as great. Orion's term 'brother' was indeed appropriate. How different was Orion from those who inhabited the Earth? Though it was obvious that Orion's life experience was completely foreign to his own, he felt a kinship, a kind of human bond. Orion looked different, a sort of Gandalf figure compared to a Hobbit, yet the affection and respect shared between these two fantasy figures were similar to what Jeremy was experiencing with his improbable friend. You couldn't make this up he thought with a wry smile.

Sadie was beginning to awaken from her deep trance state. Jeremy knew to be still and quiet while she was coming to. Any loud noises or disturbances before, during or after these sessions would jar Sadie to the point of gaining consciousness too quickly and cause her some grief. Jeremy waited until she appeared awake.

Sadie was tired, more tired than she had ever been. The juggernaut of unchecked cancer cells within her was taking its toll. She was not afraid to die. In many ways she welcomed it because she had already seen the land which she was destined to inhabit, and it was most certainly a far better place than this harsh earth. Of course, she wanted to finish her work here, especially with dear Jeremy and Orion. This desire sustained her despite the discomfort and pain which was at times acute. She did not let on to Jeremy what was going on in her body. She felt that it would just add to the burdens that he was already carrying — best to be quiet and keep the status quo, she concluded.

She wanted to go to her bed and sleep off the weight of her present condition. She felt drugged by it and knew that her spirit and stellar friends were doing their best to uphold her. She asked with insistence for Jeremy to help her to her bed, explaining that she wasn't feeling well. Jeremy kindly led her to her bed and left to resume the other chores that were waiting for him.

Life continued to make its demands on Jeremy. His work life was a stabilizing factor for him. His engagement in physical work and mental requirements helped him to steady his mood and neutralize his new worries. He continued to maintain his steady and unruffled demeanor with his customers. Muriel Phelps was reassured by this, but not his friend David as Jeremy continued to be preoccupied by his present concerns, sharing only general conversation when they were together. His mother and sister were not as alarmed as they were previously by his behavior. Things began to settle down into familiar routines for Jeremy and the world around him settled with him. Life went on and the days passed quickly.

Chapter 20

IN A PERFECT WORLD

Jeremy was eager for his next session with Sadie, but also wary of what he might learn from her regarding her physical condition and state of mind. His greatest fear was that she was tired of him and that he soon would be unwelcome in her home. Typical of the fears he carried as someone who was used to being alone, carrying the burdens of rejection. His insecurities were getting the better of him and he was angry with himself for what he realized were unsubstantiated claims swirling around in his head. If Sadie had picked up on his thoughts, she would surely grow tired of such well-worn patterns and fears.

When he entered, Sadie was neither subdued nor bedridden. She seemed her old self having started her day with a feeling that today was a blessed gifted with a return to a more energetic state. She knew that her present condition would be temporary, but today she thanked God for small miracles. She greeted Jeremy with a smile, some instructions for his usual routines in the garden and other small chores. She promised him some of his favorite soup and a hearty sandwich before their coming session with Orion. She had baked an apple pie which she knew was Jeremy's favorite as a thank you for his unerring loyalty and service towards their shared cause.

She could see the relief on Jeremy's face as she graced him with a bright smile and greeting. She knew that lately a sense of unease was building within him as he observed her declining health in the past few weeks. She was determined to change that today and the blessing of renewed well-being was indeed a gift.

Jeremy felt a great sense of relief as Sadie greeted him warmly. Maybe he was just imagining her displeasure in him. It was just another confirmation that he shouldn't read too much into another person's demeanor. You can never tell if it is your own projection or something that is real when assessing their true state. He couldn't ignore the obvious signs of Sadie's declining well-being, but he chose to leave that subject for another day.

The day went well for both of them. Jeremy was pleased with his work around Sadie's property, as both the grounds and the house looked like someone was actually living there with signs of order and beauty evident where before there was neglect and decay. He only wished that he could do the same for Sadie herself, but that was beyond his skills. She would have to fight her own battle, but he was all too willing to help her in any way that he could. He wished he could support her more but grew concerned in silence since she rarely talked about herself. Their conversations focused more on Jeremy's spiritual progress and budding understanding of spiritual life. Reviewing Orion's messages and lessons were points of discussion while Sadie explained and added to Orion's teachings as they continued to progress together.

The time for another lesson approached quickly as they ate their delicious lunch. They soon settled into their respective soft chairs. Jeremy was now well used to being surrounded by cats. Some even were quite friendly with him despite the obvious smell of dog that was never missing from his olfactory emanations. It was as if he had always been a part of their household — an adopted son who fully accepted his role as the man around the house. Though he came and went, these feline demigods were satisfied with their new subject, tolerating him well to the point of doling out some affection. Every time Orion showed up, however, the royal entourage would politely leave. They had no interest in co-mingling with this very strange entity. His odd odor repulsed them and the high pitched sounds that came from him hurt their ears. Why these humans tolerated him at all was beyond their comprehension, but there were many confusing human behaviors which they could not understand. If it wasn't for the fact that Sadie continued to serve them with food and affection, they would have left long ago.

The room was soon cleared of cats, each finding a comfortable place. They settled in far enough away from the nexus of light that was forming in the middle of the room, but close enough to be entertained by the swirling light that appeared in front of them. Orion appeared and spoke.

"I greet you once again my beautiful earth friends. Today I would like to talk about how we have come to communicate with you and answer with more details about why we chose you both as our locum of communication and focus for sharing higher laws and universal truths."

As Orion spoke, there was an aura of great authority around him, and a light which was immense. His presence was commanding as energy pulsed around him. Jeremy had never sensed Orion in this way before. Most often he came as a loving being, gentle yet firm in his expressions. Today, his presence was unmistakable, and it prompted a thread of fear within him. It was the sort of fear that comes when greeting someone who had great authority and power. Though Orion was not an entity who commanded attention in this way, Jeremy was prompted to kneel at his feet. Though he resisted that impulse, inside his mind he did just that. This sentry of light deserved nothing less. Orion proceeded to deliver yet another stunning message.

"I come more fully as myself today in hope that you will listen intently to what I have to share with you, Jeremy." It was obvious that Sadie was non compos mentis to what was taking place, yet he knew that her inner self was well aware of the situation and taking in every word.

"A series of events have led us together. It has been a somewhat circuitous route as nothing seems to take place in your world without such complications. It is important to understand that the collective light that emanates from our home world is immense and can be seen by those who are gifted with spiritual insight, though we exist many light years out into the cosmos. These emanations act as a signal to others that we are a planet that has evolved in harmony with cosmic laws and protocols fundamental to creating such light. Like you on Earth, we possess the gift of choice or freewill, but unlike your planet, my people chose the road of love from the beginning of our existence. This choice brought about benefits and manifestations of cosmic energies which helped us to develop the inherent but often dormant gifts that every soul in the Universe possesses. My people evolved quickly and almost effortlessly into what we are today. We have sustained this condition of light for many eons of time. My presence with you now is an attempt to demonstrate the beauty and spiritual power that we manifest as a result of this choice made so long ago.

"Since we emanate light, becoming a beacon in the universe, we attract many from other planets and even other galaxies. One such individual who was drawn by our light is someone you are well familiar with. His name when he walked your Earth was Yeshua Ben Joseph. He was a Jewish prophet from long ago who changed the world with love. You know him as Jesus today and he came to our world as an emissary from yours. It was a joyful meeting, one that was like long-lost cousins meeting for the first time. Jesus did not come alone, but brought with him a contingent of beautiful souls, bright and loving. We are quite capable of seeing, recognizing and communicating with spirits who are of such a high spiritual caliber, and we had no trouble acknowledging our guests. We recognized the beautiful lights emanating from He and his friends. It was apparent that because of their heightened soul development, they were able to come to our planet with no difficulty; and we recognized them immediately as truly our brothers and sisters in every respect.

"They came with a request of us to assist in what could only be described as an imminent shift of conditions on their planet that had both physical and spiritual repercussions. They explained that this shift would precipitate great change and catastrophic events that would test all who inhabit Earth mightily. Extreme changes such as this are exceedingly rare in the cosmos. They usually happen after many millions of years of evolution in conjunction with a conflagration of cosmic energies precipitating such fundamental shifts. They worried for their people who inhabited the material plane and the immensity of what was about to happen. They sought help from outside their planet in the hope that greater resources could be applied that would ease the blow of this change. Hence, they came to us utilizing their knowledge of spiritual laws in order to find us and to communicate.

"We accepted their invitation without hesitation and plans were set into motion in order for us to respond effectively to our brethren's request. It was not merely the result of our collective planning and efforts, however. Like all spiritually attuned souls in the cosmos, we relied upon divine guidance and help. We had quickly come to realize that there was a divine plan regarding what was to happen on planet Earth. Indeed, all parties concerned had their role to play in this plan, as do you Jeremy. Do you really believe that our meeting and its outcomes are the result of a random act? Certainly not! Would you believe that God had a plan for you even before you entered into your world? The divine plan has been set in motion for hundreds of years involving many thousands of souls, culminating in the work that we are doing at this moment. Though you are not alone in this venture but, in fact, you are one of many hundreds that God has seeded with a purpose and role to play. As with anything that reflects divine intention and manifestation, many seeds are planted, some on fertile and some on barren ground. There is great latitude for error and success, especially when involving such an intransigent world as yours.

"The seed of possibility that is you my dear fellow, as well as your beautiful teacher whom I speak through, has responded well to the divine call; and you are growing accordingly. Though the law of freewill has its influence and part to play in this venture, you have both responded exceedingly well thus far. Planning and effort to guide you both together has been a very complex matter. Many advanced beings on many levels of existence have contributed to this desired outcome. It is unfortunate, but less than 5% of those chosen so far have responded in an overt way. Thus, our appreciation and commitment to you both is tremendous. You represent the most worthy and we will guard and protect you without exception. You are crucial to the success of the divine plan as we all follow divine will which is well understood by us and those cohorts from your world that we are partnering with.

"I know that at times you are bewildered and mystified about why you have been chosen for such an important role. The simple explanation is that you are destined. A more complex answer is that within your true essence there are many gifts and abilities that you are yet to be aware of. The being that is truly you is hidden by a mind and many spiritual impediments that prevent you from understanding your true self. We are putting in a great deal of effort to help you open to those potentials that are within. Indeed, you are on an intensive program to accomplish this task. Few have experienced such support as this; and you are a very blessed man.

"In our next session, I will elaborate on coming events that will contribute to the great changes that are expected in the near future. We are not investing our time and effort for you alone Jeremy. We intend to assist you to higher consciousness and expression of your gifts so that you will become a leader and great comforter for many during this time of transition. For now, I urge you not to ruminate too much on what your future might look like. Rather, focus on your lessons and prayers. Now is the time for preparation and self-discovery, not to jump the gun as you say, entering into your role prematurely and unprepared."

Orion bid good day to his hosts with the intent of returning at the appointed hour in one week's time. He urged Jeremy to continue to open himself to the Divine, receiving the crucial essence that he talked about, and to deeply consider Orion's words. He promised that Jeremy would never be alone during their time apart as he had many spirit helpers and celestial angels by his side. Sadie was also very much in the picture, willing to help him with his various questions.

Orion left Sadie, exhaling a disjointed breath that included a rather loud snort as she came to. Rather than extreme fatigue, she felt refreshed and a sense of expansiveness derived from Orion's overshadowing. If she could feel this way every day, she would be happy to continue the work indefinitely. She knew, however, that there was a definite timeline that could not be changed. That brought her down a bit, but not enough to erase her mood.

Jeremy too felt a sense of elation. Although he also felt a knot in his stomach that was a response to Orion's personal message to him. The drug of love which was so much in the air when Orion was present continued to lift him up with its strange hypnotic effect. They were both on a high and wanted to stay there forever. As always, reality struck soon enough as the pressures of the outside world forced their way into their consciousness. Nonetheless, both Jeremy and Sadie felt the afterglow of their time together infusing the following week with a lightness of being that was most pleasurable. In contrast, the tone of the next session with Orion was very different indeed.

Chapter 21

COMING TO GRIPS

Jeremy was beginning to wake up to a very different reality than what he had known. His emotional life was deeper than ever, sometimes feeling unfamiliar sensations well up from within. His old patterns of suppressing or even ignoring his feelings were contradicted by a deeper state, an inner truth that insisted on being acknowledged and expressed without any form of censorship. This moment was no exception as he felt tears form and run down his cheeks — a bittersweet reflection of the duality he was feeling. Tears welled up as he sensed his soul's destiny mixed with joy. A state of laughter and pain was confusing, but an accurate reflection of his feelings as he grappled with the new reality forming inside him. His life was no longer simple or straightforward. It was replaced with concepts and perceptions that broadened and enlightened his understanding of the world. He never sought out this knowledge, and yet it was manifesting with each day.   He, on one hand, lived a seemingly normal life, yet his inner world was far from normal.

His feelings as a stranger in a strange land deepened. He saw his actions and the actions of others as an expression of the somnambulant state preventing everyone around him from waking up to the inconsistencies and contradictions of modern life. He instinctively knew that the gift of life was being squandered by so many. This was the price of unhappiness so many paid for social compliance and material stability. He felt a deep sadness for his brothers and sisters realizing how trapped everyone was. Although he too was in the game, he felt with his continued soul growth and newfound perceptions that he would find a way to break free from the web of falsehoods and deception he could now see all around him. For now, he would play it cool, and follow Orion's and Sadie's directions to practice love and tolerance.

He tried talking to those who meant the most to him. His mother Judy and sister Megan were nonplussed by his attempt to educate them. Even Muriel Phelps was once again concerned for Jeremy's well-being. She wondered whether her advice to seek out Sadie's council was such a good idea. She knew that they were spending an inordinate amount of time together, but certainly didn't believe the rumors circulating around town that they were lovers. The improbability of this put a smile on her face since she knew both of them well enough to reject such nonsense.

Though she had her own thoughts about what they were up to, she kept her ideas to herself for now. She knew there was something seriously wrong with Sadie since she had not been herself the last time they were together. Sadie was a private person and Muriel respected her and did not pry. Muriel was sensitive enough to pick up on her unspoken troubles, it brought many thoughts and speculations to mind, adding to Muriel's list of concerns around Jeremy and Sadie's deepening relationship.

Jeremy's friend David was almost grief-stricken with the complete shift he saw in Jeremy. His old friend seemed distant and lacking engagement when they got together for their usual Saturday night beer and chin wag. He wondered what he had done to cause his friend to be so distant. While David often carried the conversation when they were together, he felt his words were unheard. Though his friend nodded and gestured in the right places, Jeremy wouldn't interject his own thoughts other than commenting about the world coming to an end. He's losing it big time, thought David, as he yet again let Jeremy expound on the troubles of the world, and how humanity was asleep at the wheel.

David had his own theories of a world controlled by a cabal of only twelve individuals; and working for the man was accepting their control of your life. Yes, he knew that the world was in trouble. The daily news harped on this fact continually. Everyone knew that the problems of the world were insurmountable, but Jeremy's idea that aliens in cahoots with angels were going to solve our problems was a crock. No go with David, Jeremy thought as he once again saw David's eyes glaze over when he shared his latest discoveries about what was in store for planet Earth.

Jeremy felt more alone than ever. His only true friend was Sadie and by association, Orion. Most times he felt as if he was in a corner with no way out, though at other times, skyrocketing into a new and amazing awareness that brought a deep sense of joy and understanding. Jeremy, the human was slowly fading. Orion and Sadie talked about soul transformation and how necessary it was for him to engage in this process, but experiencing it was not at all what he expected. Rather than trusting in his five senses and intellect to make sense of the world, a different set of faculties were contributing to this process in ways that were often disturbing and disorienting. Every day brought more changes in perceptions, shifting him from his familiar reality to something entirely unfamiliar. As he continued his daily routines and interactions, he could sense the real thoughts of others, often contradicting their spoken words, revealing a private inner world that he was uncomfortable witnessing. He heard a lot of judgments, fears, and inability to truly acknowledge and listen. It was an inner dialogue that was completely different from what was spoken. It was like an intricate game of hide and seek with an intention of being seen and heard by others but, that seeing was far from what was happening.

It was all too confusing for Jeremy as he felt incapable, at least consciously of playing the game. He said what he meant to say and felt, but also saw that others very often misinterpreted his actions and his intentions. They were reading from a different playbook, and this contributed to his deep sense of separation. At times, his crazy thoughts of the inconsistencies between his inner world and the outer world were intensifying daily.

He longed to be in the room with Sadie and Orion. There, everything made sense. It was real, not reshaped by a distorted mirror image. He felt safe and comfortable with his friends. They understood him while the rest of the world was on such a different wavelength that there was no understanding or acceptance. He was either going crazy or seeing the world for what it is. Either way, it was scary and filled him with dread. He felt weak inside, wanting to turn back the clock to the time before he met Orion on the mountain. There was no turning back. He knew that life had changed forever. He began to understand how strong Sadie was, acknowledging how others judged her and her differences, yet she remained herself. At least she saw him for who he was and did not judge him. In fact, he knew that she loved him and he loved her. She had become mother, friend, and confidant — something that he had never truly had in his life. Yet, she asked little of him other than his generosity and willingness to provide for her needs. He appreciated the no-nonsense way about her. It grounded him and helped make sense of his ever changing inner world. Cloaking all of this was the surety of a mother's love — one that had his back and truly saw him as he is. Together, they made a formidable team, tackling a resistance innate in humanity, restricting and perverting the truth in a world gone a little mad. Together, they were determined to crack the egg of resistance, allowing the sweetness of soul to rise above the fray, and to live the truth as best they could — a prospect that was both exhilarating and terrifying.

Jeremy had been deeply concerned with what the world thought of him before he began this journey, but now felt immune to its judgments. A little of Sadie had rubbed off on him, and he was determined to live freely in his own expression of truth and authenticity. Rather than be afraid, he felt courage and determination well up from his core. He relished the idea of applying his newfound self in every situation. The old Jeremy had to take a back seat to the juggernaut of his new self, emerging with every breath. He was a changed man still in the throes of transformation. Though he was circumspect with those close to him, he was determined to be authentic to his true self, not allowing the old Jeremy to have his way. This did not go unnoticed by others. His new confidence and forthrightness were all too apparent. Before, he would rarely express an opinion with a client; now he was liberal with his perceptions.

Some loved this new Jeremy, while others were displeased. Those who were only interested in hearing themselves talk were dismayed when Jeremy interjected commentary that reflected his newfound wisdom. He felt judgment coming his way, but it did not stop him from speaking his truth. He even lost a few clients as a result of his exuberance, but he was unperturbed. He felt joy as he perceived the unfolding world in its new light. He felt a deep love welling up within him — a love that was much less conditional and more generous in expression. Along with this love, rose compassion and joy. He was experiencing the effects of God's touch as the divine essence was flowing into him in ever increasing quantities. Each time this happened during a prayer, asking to receive the essence, the inner joy increased and the stamina to navigate the changes he was experiencing helped steady him on the journey.

He worried much less for the world that was on the brink. He was realizing that the change he was experiencing would someday soon be common to many others. The coming upheaval must first happen internally before the external storm. That way, he would be able to navigate through it without being lost at sea. In his euphoria, Jeremy could not fathom the depth that he and humanity would be tested. The consequences of humanity's actions over eons, characterized by a self-determined path, would create such a whirlwind of responses that no one would be immune. He could imagine that the world would be turned upside down, and it would be anyone's guess as to who would emerge as survivors and leaders in the new world prophesied by Orion. He thought of Bobby Dylan's words: "The last will be first and the first will be last for the times they are a-changing," was an apt description of coming times.

He realized that the lack of humility and extreme ignorance of the universal laws that govern harmony will result in serious consequences; and very few people are aware of the impending danger.

Today, Jeremy did not entertain those types of thought for long as he immersed himself in a world with only love and joy in his heart. He was determined to hold on to his reverie and let tomorrow bring what will. He sensed that such happiness could not last forever, but in this moment, he soared with a soul captured by God's love feeling like he was the happiest man on Earth. Though there may be doom and gloom on the horizon, this sunlit day will have none of it. He felt freedom from life's burdens so intense that he wasn't sure if his feet were touching the ground. If this is the life God intends for everyone, then he was happy to discover its sweetness today, hoping never to return to the heaviness of the old world.

Chapter 22

FORECAST FOR THE FUTURE

In Madison, late September days were getting crisp and damp, foreshadowing the onset of fall and the darker days of winter to come. Jeremy's outdoor work was speeding up as he labored to put his client's gardens to sleep for the season. Unfortunately, his personal dilemmas were not abating with the season. His world was becoming more bizarre and surprising than ever. He dreamed often of conversations between him and Orion about his role as a light bringer, Orion's term. Orion advised Jeremy that in order to fulfill his destiny, he needed to let go of his biases and expectations regarding his future. He could rely on the Universal source to take care of the details if he accepted and followed the guidance. God had a plan and Jeremy was urged to follow along, exercising what was clearly an act of faith.

"Faith in what?" Jeremy thought. How could he have faith in a future that looked apocalyptic? How could he have faith in himself when who he was in the past was now irrelevant?' Life was changing so fast that he felt there was no solid ground beneath him. He was riding the winds of inner change without any sense of where it was taking him. He was usually stubborn and sometimes intractable to change. He understood it would take courage and stamina to trust the direction he was taking, but he was committed to the challenge.

Juggling the real with the unreal inner world had become more challenging with each day. He felt trapped without a way out, but he also felt a blooming sense of inner joy. He was experiencing the challenges that most true spiritual seekers encounter — a conflict between the linear mind and the multi-dimensional soul mind. Sadie warned him about this; but he didn't truly understand it until he was in the midst of it. This was the hardest thing he had ever encountered in his life. It deeply hurt but felt blissfully good at the same time. The contradictions of living in faith were becoming increasingly clear. He was not losing himself as he feared; but was coming to know himself in ways that were foreign, yet authentic. He thought of the schizophrenic who had more than one personal reality. If he were to reveal his present mental state to the outside world, he too could be judged as mentally unstable.

He understood why people like Sadie were condemned and ostracized. Heck, if he didn't have these experiences himself, he would join them in their opinions and ignorance. He remembered his own fears and judgments about Sadie before he really got to know her. He wondered how many others in the world shared this odd reality, lacking in verifiable fact and material proof of its existence. He took comfort in the fact that he was still able to work, something that always grounded him. Strangely, he was not afraid of the future, rather, his inner sense told him that things would work out for him and that there was no turning back. Instead, he girded his loins and forged ahead.

His anticipation of their next session with Orion was an amalgam of fear and excitement. He wanted to know more about what was coming down the pike. But true to form, he didn't want to know what might happen to him if it included a painful and premature demise. Yet he was determined to engage with Orion as requested. Sadie was again not feeling her best. Jeremy had to be content with leftover soup, a bit of cheese, and some stale bread. Not her usual love offering. Jeremy put his concerns aside to prepare for their session with Orion.

Sadie said her prayer as usual and the atmosphere in the room changed in response.

"My dear friends spoke Orion. It is indeed a pleasure to be with you once again. You feel a deep anticipation within you regarding what I have to share today. I will be discussing what I see as the human condition. We have spoken of this before, but my words today will act as a segue to the main points I wish to make later. I will compare our social structures to yours as a way of illustrating why conditions on Earth are in need of severe recalibration.

"On my planet we work for the benefit of all. We are divided into segments or cells which are a part of the whole. Each group forms a unique component which fits harmoniously with all other components in the wider community and extrapolates further into society as a whole. Each member of the collective finds their place within it. This reflects their individual gifts and attributes, combining with others to make an effective and beautiful contribution to the whole, thus complementing the entire community structure. Work, as you define it, does not exist on my planet. We are not engaged enough in our endeavors to cause great stress to our emotional and physical state. We are happy in our work and engage in it often, as it reflects our love for life and one another. It fulfills us and it carries us into further realms of endeavors and contributions as we evolve within it. There is no end to what might be accomplished through our contributions to the social network. We live a long and productive life serving the whole in whatever way that reflects our true selves and gifts. This may seem a utopian life to those of you who live on Earth, but such a place can be within your grasp once you come to understand the love principles that are so much a part of our world.

"In contrast, your world is a very different place. Love is not the cohesive force as it is in ours. Certainly, it does exist, but the form of love expressed is often a dim reflection of the innate love which every soul in the Universe has the capacity to express. There are unfortunately many other aspects of human expression which are more predominant. I need not list all of the undesirable expressions of the human psyche that I'm sure you know very well. Their expressions have influenced and guided human progression through the ages. Rather than love as a key component of human motivation, the desire for power, control, wealth, and status seems to be the primary directive in many parts of your world.

Few are able to break free of these directives. Your communication through various channels and devices constantly reinforces these attitudes. You are programmed to follow such patterns of thought and behavior. Psychically, every individual broadcasts their thoughts into the atmosphere. Thoughts are real and they have the power to influence. Not only are there material forms of human intention and expression, but there are also great currents of psychic thought forms that cover the Earth.

"There are other forms of human influence and conditioning that are not well understood and quite subtle, yet very powerful. Since psychic energies possess real power, we are noticing another source that generates and reinforces human thought and behavior. It is the direct expression of discarnate humanity known to you as spirits. They are directing a vast amount of thought influence on all who inhabit the Earth. This influence has both positive and negative outcomes in human endeavors because both intentions are expressed by various spirits who surround humanity. The laws governing this are complex, and I will not go into detail. It is important to know that thought attracts many sources of influence at all times. The mind is a great generator and sponge capable of engaging these energetic components that circle your globe. The law of attraction ensures that what you sow, think, and act upon, you also reap, attracting a great spectrum of thought influence from many sources. These influences reinforce your thinking and motivations to a great extent, though you are most often unaware of their source and intent. Consequently, it is a double-edged sword that can precipitate both positive and negative outcomes within your thinking and resulting decisions.

"The world is caught up in a vicious cycle of action and reaction that is continually reinforced by one's thoughts, motivations, and outside influences. No one is immune from this situation but some, such as yourself, have drawn you to powerful forces that exert enough light and clarity to help generate a form of protection around you. You are the lucky few who have drawn beautiful energies into your midst. You benefit from a form of immunity from the dark and contrary conditions that are ever-present in your world. In order for you to know the bigger picture about why your world is so caught up in these disharmonious conditions, I have given you this preamble.

"Now, I want to speak of what may come of this world so out of sync with universal laws that govern love and harmony. Every action has its consequences and reactions, and this too is a law. For those poor souls who believe that their actions, whether good or bad, will not suffer the fate of future and definitive consequences are sorely mistaken.

"On a global level, your world at this time is smothered in darkness. Very few of you earthlings perceive this as truth because your senses are focused merely on your physical reality. Indeed, you suffer, and your thoughts and perceptions reflect your limited viewpoint. But you are also experiencing dark conditions on spiritual levels that you do not often understand or acknowledge.

"Jeremy, my friend, you are opening up in your awareness in a limited way, but as you grow and develop, more things will become clear. For now, you have the sensation of experiencing two worlds at once. This is a temporary consequence to the awakening of soul consciousness. This dichotomy is caused by a different source of consciousness or perceived reality that is both disorienting and often contrary to the mind's perception of worldly reality. All people must come to that place of wakefulness in time, and the time approaches when conditions will help precipitate this awakening, at least in some. How this will take place is of great consequence to every soul on your planet.

"We have witnessed this process on occasion in other planetary systems, and it is a most fascinating event. Unfortunately, your planet is dying, not from cosmic forces, but from human endeavors that are sapping the lifeblood out of her. As a result, cosmic systems and forces present since the beginning of time are now being activated in order to return your planet to a pristine state. There is a cosmic law dictating that all things must pursue balance and harmony. This does not mean that humanity is to be snuffed out by the angry hand of God, as your ancestors often thought. No, the end of the world is not nigh; rather a new beginning is about to be gifted to humanity. A beginning that will be imposed one way or another.

"Since the vast majority of humanity is sleepwalking through life, what is coming will not only startle them, but also terrify them because of the extraordinary results of these interventions. Yes, it will feel like the end of the world for many, and indeed it will be the end of the world as you know it, as the illusions will be shattered and a new reality emerges.

"The consequences resulting from collective human actions will collide with the cosmic forces impacting human constructs and creations on your planet that will be violent and disruptive. The time of human domination, ignoring long-term consequences in favor of short-term gains, will soon be over. Humanity will observe true power in all its forms as cosmic laws are enacted to bring about greater harmony. Nothing and no one will be immune from these consequences as the world capitulates to divine order. So we come to those like yourself to warn and educate about what is to come.

"I think that I will leave you now so that you are able to absorb what I have shared with you. I will continue my message the next time we meet. May the blessings of love be with you my dear friends."

At that, Orion left the room leaving behind a disappointed Jeremy who was looking forward to some hard facts surrounding Orion's serious pronouncements. But he would have to wait until next time.

Sadie again was very tired. She couldn't hide it from Jeremy, and she saw the look of concern on his face as she came out of her trance. Her eyes were sunken and bloodshot, and her skin blotchy and pale. Usually, after their sessions with Orion, she was uplifted and refreshed. This time was just the opposite, and it showed. She realized that soon she had to tell him the reasons for her ill health, and she dreaded it. But the truth needed to be spoken sooner or later and she supposed that now was as good a time as any.

Chapter 23

THE NEWS

"Are you alright Sadie?" Jeremy asked with a deep look of concern on his face.

"Unfortunately, I am not", she responded with her usual directness. "I have a condition which I have been meaning to tell you about for some time now. I have lymphoma, a type of cancer of the blood that is fatal if not treated, she said straight faced with great dignity. Please don't mention that I need to go into treatment. As you may have guessed, the doctors are very firm about my seeking medical treatment."

Jeremy was stunned, shaken in fact by the news of his dear friend's imminent demise. He struggled to understand Sadie's position. Life is sacred he thought, and she should do whatever possible to uphold life. But he knew Sadie well enough that when she made up her mind about something, she was intractable in her position. He felt helpless and his inability to say something prompted Sadie to go on.

"I've lived a good life Jeremy," she said with deep sincerity. It is not a life that most would choose, but one that has been meaningful and on my own terms. Although my time may be short, I want to continue to live this life to the end with dignity. What I need most is your support and, hopefully, to be with me when it is my time to pass over. For now, I'm determined to stay the course until I can no longer stand the pain. I've made arrangements and have put my house in order, she said with a mixture of pride and self-assurance. You need not worry about my fate young man. Instead, you need to worry about your own, which is most important right now. My problems are my own, but I want to assure you that I will do whatever I can to uphold our project together. I know that Orion is counting on us to keep forging ahead; and I know that I have received an abundance of healing in order to fulfill my part in the matter," she said with all sincerity. I'm not a quitter, Jeremy but there comes a time when things must come to its conclusion and that time is soon."

"My unconventional life has been filled with blessings and I wouldn't have it any other way. As a woman, I've not followed the prescribed role of wife and mother. There are some regrets there but not enough to feel that I've lost out in a big way. Instead, I've devoted my life in service to others and personal inner growth. Not that I've been a saint, I've certainly had my dalliances and experimented with various lifestyles, but in the end, all of these experiences have brought me to where I am today. No regrets whatsoever! Through my faith, God has provided me with untold blessings, some that might otherwise never have been realized. There is no greater happiness than having deep meaning and purpose to one's life. Helping others find their way has benefited me in so many ways. Letting go of society's conventions came at a price, but it has been well worth the pain of rejection and judgment from all those who are barely awake. On the other hand, I have met such interesting people, including you Jeremy, and they have added such spice to my life. My spiritual journey has gifted me with insight and soul awareness in so many ways that I could not count how God has blessed and lifted me beyond the confines of human perception. I now view life with a combination of joy and wisdom, something that few have come to recognize and live by. That is the great gift my soul in communion with my Creator has given me. His love has healed and transformed me into who I am today. I have no fear of passing over, my friend, instead, I welcome it and death welcomes me. I'm ready any time because I know without a shadow of a doubt where I'm going and compared to this harsh world, it is truly paradise. So don't grieve for me Jeremy; be happy that I've had a fulfilling life and that the life beyond will be another exciting chapter in this never-ending journey." Sadie declared with fierceness, an emotion that he had not seen in her for some time.

Though Sadie could feel herself fading with each day, her Appalachian stoicism kept her from faltering in the face of such great difficulties. She was determined to give this journey her best fight to the bitter end, but also felt comfort in leaving her fate in the hands of God. She felt deeply that what had begun with Jeremy would find its desired conclusion. For now, she had faith that they would continue with their extraordinary journey together with Orion at the helm.

Tears welled up in Jeremy's eyes as the full extent of the news sunk in. He would be losing his best friend, one who was both a mother and mentor to him. By merely contemplating this, he felt the pain of this impending loss acutely. How could he cope without her he thought with a tinge of panic in his gut? She had become his rock and saving grace, and so much a part of his life that he couldn't imagine it without her.

His tears turned into sobs. The very thought of losing her was unbearable, but there before him was the truth that he could not deny. "What am I going to do," he blurted out in a plaintive expression of deep concern.

"Oh come now Jeremy, it's not the end of the world dear boy, she expressed with part exasperation and part sympathy for what she knew would be difficult for him to accept. "For God's sake, I'm not dead yet," she exclaimed in an attempt to clear the air! I'm sure that we will have a lot more time together and enough time to finish what we have started. In fact, I'm counting on it," she huffed with reassurance. "Pull yourself together Jeremy," her old self coming to the fore as she put one hand on his shoulder for comfort.

She disliked emotional raw displays such as this. It reminded her of how her mother and aunts used to caterwaul with grief every time someone in the family passed away. She didn't want to join him in his tears, but being sensitive as she was, it took everything she had to not go there.

Finally, his tears lessened and stopped. Jeremy was embarrassed by his outburst, but he couldn't help it. He loved her so deeply, and the relationship that they shared changed his life in so many ways. The thought of not having her steady and wise hand to help him in his precarious journey to awaken spiritually was unbearable. He thought that he had better go because it was obvious that he was not supporting her or staying strong and steady for her. He resolved to end the conversation with a quick exit. He realized that he was not doing either of them any good by sticking around and commiserating in his grief over her future demise. He had to get out of there so that he could grieve without upsetting her, and hopefully pull himself together.

He hugged her goodbye and fled. Sadie was sorry that she shared the grim truth with him, but she knew that she could not put it off any longer. So, the cat is out of the bag now, she thought with a tinge of remorse coupled with a sense that she did what she needed to do. Her worry was that this news would change everything, and that Jeremy would lose focus on the task at hand. All she could do was wait to see how Jeremy would process the news and find a way to cope. She thought with a deep sigh and sense of acceptance, what will be, will be. Next Tuesday will tell the tale. She was sure of that, and she hoped for the best. She wondered why people were so afraid of death. It was just another chapter in the book of life and, in her case, she thought of it as a welcome event. She very much wanted Jeremy to see things from her perspective, but she knew that his neediness and lack of spiritual maturity would prevent him from doing so.

She thought no more of their discussion since she had many things to attend to, the least of which was to change her will. She had an appointment to see Charles Fearing, the lawyer, tomorrow and had to get her paperwork together in preparation for the meeting. Life goes on, she thought. Yes, life goes on.

Chapter 24

THE NEW REALITY

The burden of Sadie's news fell heavily on Jeremy's thoughts and heart. He thought about how easily he had missed the signs that would have told him the truth quite some time ago. Yet, he knew that he would only see what his heart would let him, and he certainly didn't want to recognize this sad reality. He felt betrayed by God who set him on this journey with Sadie and Orion. Was it all about to end? He was confused and worried about how he would be able to continue with their project without Sadie's gifts. It felt like a disaster was looming in front of him, not knowing when things would fall apart. Oh, how bittersweet life can be, he thought with a wistful sigh.

He found solace in his work. It kept his mind off of those burning questions that haunted his thoughts and dreams. The physicality of his work helped to numb his overactive brain, and at the end of the day, forced much-needed sleep his body required, giving him much needed peace. He was a mess, but he was coping better than he thought. Besides, as Sadie aptly pointed out, I'm not dead yet, he mused as he worked. This gave him a measure of comfort, and he resolved to make the best of their time together. He was going to take one day at a time, and use that day to continue to mine the depths of spiritual truth that Sadie helped him to understand. He didn't want to waste his time considering the emptiness that would ensue with Sadie's passing. He had to be strong and wise about what was coming and with these thoughts, he felt an inner affirmation that he was on the right track.

Muriel Phelps certainly noticed the change in Jeremy's demeanor. That man is up and down like a yo-yo. One day, he was almost delirious with joy, and the next down in the dumps. She was sure that Sadie Jenkins had something to do with his present state, and she was determined to ask him about it.

Upon their usual Monday greeting, she blurted out her question. "You don't look so good today, Jeremy," she said with obvious concern. "Are you alright my dear?"

"I'm fine Muriel, in a tone that said otherwise. I've just heard some bad news that I wasn't expecting, and it has thrown me for a bit of a loop."

"It's about Sadie Jenkins, isn't it Jeremy?"

How did you know, Jeremy asked with bewilderment?

"Just a feeling Jeremy, just a feeling, she repeated with the look of a sage. I haven't heard much from her lately. Since we would often take tea together at her home and chat about our lives — not seeing her recently raised a few suspicions", commented Muriel with a hint of a coy look on her face. "Is she ill Jeremy?"

With glassy eyes, he confirmed her suspicions. "Unfortunately, there is nothing that can be done for Sadie. I've tried to persuade her to seek help, but she refuses. She wants to die in peace and there is nothing any of us can do about it." Tears were now flowing down his cheeks.

"Oh, dear boy, what sad news this is." She too was feeling very emotional. As an elder, she could understand Sadie's perspective, but she felt tremendous sympathy for Jeremy's plight as well. She knew that they had grown very close over the past few months." Although I know that you can't interfere with another person's private life, I'm sure that you tried your best to dissuade her from her present course of action, she expressed with deep sorrow. What else can you do dear boy? She's following her heart, and it's a very important life choice that can only be hers to make."

"I know Muriel, and Sadie said as much, but oh how I wish that we were not in this boat, her and I. There is nothing I would want more than to have more time together. She is my lifeline these days, and she's filled my life up with experiences and things I could never have imagined," he said with a longing that rose deep from his soul.

"Is it Sadie that brought you these experiences, or could it be God using her to reach you?" Muriel asked in her wisdom. "You know, God uses many avenues and people to touch the seeking soul. He brought you to Sadie and I'm sure that He will bring you to others who will help you on your journey. You just have to be open to the idea and have faith that you are being looked after."

Jeremy couldn't fully entertain this idea yet, as the grief was too fresh. But she had a point. He realized that everything that had happened so far was not only extraordinary, but God guided as well. In time, he knew that new avenues and possibilities would open up for him in surprising ways. Yes, Muriel was right, having faith in the future was all he had to give him strength, and so he must forge on trusting in the will and plan that God had for him.

"Thank you, Muriel, for your support and understanding," he said with the sincere honesty — a trait that was very dear to Muriel. "I feel better for talking to you about this, and I know that she is a good friend of yours as well. I hope that I haven't upset you too much with this news," he said with a loving look that was Jeremy to the core.

"Don't worry, Jeremy. I would have found out eventually anyway. You know how that old dear loves to keep her secrets. Now I can offer my support in some way, and I will. And if you get in trouble for telling me the truth, remember, I forced it out of you!" she said with a wink and a nod.

At that they carried on with their day. This conversation brought them even closer — allied with support and knowledge that they are there for each other despite what might happen with Sadie.

Chapter 25

When he entered Sadie's home that Tuesday, Sadie was relieved to see him composed and even cheerful. This turnaround in Jeremy's demeanor was a welcome gift on a day that started with few physical symptoms, and an inner cheerfulness that brightened her day. To see Jeremy also with a positive outlook confirmed that through outside support, Orion and others were propping her up with healing energies and light balms which lessened the pain considerably.

Sadie had told him that he need not continue with his reclamation project around the house. What he had accomplished over these past months was nothing short of a miracle, and she was well satisfied with the results. "Besides," she said with great confidence, "I've just been to the lawyers and changed my will. You are to inherit everything I own, Jeremy, including the house. It's not much, but it is my hope that it will help you in the future to have an easier life. You can do what you want with it, but I ask that you to make sure every cat either finds a good home or you will find a way to look after them for me. I trust that you will take my wishes seriously and not ignore them. It is very important to me that when I'm gone, you will take care of all that is very dear to me. Jeremy, you are the closest thing I have to family now. For now, our time together is better spent by communicating with Orion, and continuing with your spiritual education," she declared in her usual clipped manner designed to circumvent any protests from Jeremy. "Besides", she said, " you can't take it with you, can you?"

Jeremy was stunned by her declarations. He felt a sense of shame because he had not known her for that long, yet she was willing to give him everything she had upon her demise. What an odd person she was, but one who was always clear of mind and soul he thought. He knew not to argue with her as this only perturbed her. Instead, he nodded and continued to listen, although his mind was racing with questions and thoughts.

Sadie's usual forthrightness dampened the mood a bit. He knew that his efforts around the place always brightened Sadie's spirits and it was one way he could support her. Yet, now he understood that everything could wait until there was time to put things into perspective. To think of this place without Sadie in it was a bit overwhelming, and he forced the thought out of his mind. He wanted their time together to be uplifting and full of good intentions with all the blessings that came with it. He could also appreciate why she wanted to focus less on material concerns; and it made a lot of sense to be fully engaged in the work at hand. After his talk with Muriel, he realized that feeling sorry for him and Sadie would not do any good. It was time to make the most of the situation and do as Sadie suggested. He was eager to follow her lead and comply with her wishes. Rather than taking up where he left off with home projects, he settled into having a conversation with his dear friend, thinking that he must remember these moments and treasure them in times to come.

They talked about many things. Sadie would ask him about how he viewed the world differently now he knew so very little about the spiritual world surrounding him. He told her in detail about how his perceptions were changing, and how odd it was to be living in what seemed like a dual universe. He shared his thoughts describing a demonstrable version of the quantum universe where duality lived side by side without contradictions.

His life had become stranger than fiction because of his chance encounter with an alien on a mountaintop and the medium he sought to confirm or dispel his experience. He could never tell his friends or loved ones the entire truth about how these experiences had forged an entirely new perspective within him. He knew they couldn't possibly relate to it. He had to live within this reality in order to understand it; otherwise, the experience lacked context and a sense of reality. His reality had been transformed, its indelible mark made him into something he would not have recognized a year ago. He was becoming almost as alien as Orion. This realization left a hollow feeling in his gut, yet there was also joy residing there. It's duality bittersweet.

Sadie appreciated every nuance of his descriptions and experiences, as she too had traveled the same road. Her experiences on that road were unique to her, but there were enough common markers on the way to confirm the route. It was wonderful for her to have someone else confirm this road less traveled, and to talk about it so openly, as the two of them have done with each other. Their unique souls were blossoming in their own way, appreciating the wonder contained in each other, and confirming a unique bond that was so unusual in their lives. It was a love that flourished as their souls grew in the blessings of God's Love.

It was time to open the door for Orion to come and share further revelations. They readied themselves and the room so that he could enter through the portal that was created by their prayers and desires. He arrived wearing a mantle of golden light announcing his presence and filling the room with peace.

"I come again to be with you", my friends, he said in his distinct baritone voice. "I wish to add more to my previous message and to respond in greater detail about what we perceive as the coming events that will change your world irrevocably.

"As I stated previously, your world is in a deep crisis, and so many have not recognized this very serious issue. Humanity is like a frog sitting in a pot of warm water, enjoying and feeling content despite the fact that the pot is heating up from a formidable flame beneath it. The frog will not leave the pot because of the pleasure it derives from bathing in its warmth, and it continues to drift into a state of extreme relaxation that pulsates through its body. Lulled by pleasure, he is oblivious to his fate.

Yet, if he does not leave, inevitably the frog will be scalded to death. So it is with humanity. You continue to enjoy the pleasures of your world, exploiting all that it has to offer, unable to look beyond this superficiality to perceive the dangers that are fomenting.

Blind ignorance has driven most human behavior for a very long time. It has caused wars, great suffering, and disharmony throughout the ages. Now you are enjoying some of the fruits of your labors manifest through much human ingenuity. It has brought abundance and many physical comforts to your lives. The frog sits contentedly in the pot, but the time approaches rapidly for the pot to boil over. How many will escape? Knowledge combined with wise actions may have prevented much of this looming catastrophe. Unfortunately, few have heeded the warning signs, and those who have the power to bring change have turned a blind eye to the situation. The vast majority of humanity will be subject to the negative consequences of willful ignorance and blindness. It is an ignorance that can be blissful, but exacts painful consequences.

You have constructed a very complex system for living on your planet. It is comprised of many interdependencies and systems that have brought great material benefits to your daily living. You have become dependent on what we see as a very fragile and vulnerable framework for life. The linkage of various systems is weak and based on certain assumptions of economic and cultural norms. These assumptions depend upon flawed logic reflecting mindful paradigms expanded through social programming and engineering. One can assume that the interconnected components of this complex system are linked by corrupt and inaccurate paradigms developed quickly and haphazardly in a very short timeframe, instead of a sound understanding of universal dynamics. Your present culture is immature compared to eons of human history, and the collapse of your present systems is inevitable. It is the parable of the house built on sand, vulnerable to the shifting tides that are being played out by humanity. The flawed nature of your endeavors interacting with natural systems that sustain your Earth is being disrupted as a result of the sheer weight of human endeavors upon them. The pot continues to heat up as a consequence of flawed human perception, and behavior and is soon to reach its boiling point.

Your systems are vulnerable in many ways to these disruptions unable to stand up to major shifts that can manifest in a multitude of ways. Climate change, solar flares, wars, earthquakes, tsunamis, volcanic eruptions, and destructive fires, combined with pandemics and social disorder, could topple your systems and become irreparable. The dominoes are in place and with one major push, the flattening will begin. If you have faith that your government will be able to repair the damage and restore order, you are sadly mistaken. Once major systems are damaged, many other tertiary systems will follow until there is nothing to sustain your economy and social constructs. You will find yourselves naked and vulnerable to the changing tides of life on Mother Earth.

You probably wonder what would sustain you if all this were to happen. We are eager to teach you how to cope with such upheavals. We see that this time can bring about the possibility of great change and recalibration for the better, while upholding and enhancing human life on Earth. There is a vast and crucial plan in place to help humanity recover from the onslaught of destruction and change. It will not be done through a coordinated effort by your present governments. Rather, it will happen through what you call grassroots efforts established in various pockets throughout the globe. We are participants in this plan as are many others, not only from other planets in the galaxy, but also those who are from other dimensions associated with your world. There are beautiful souls who once lived on Earth, but have progressed far beyond its present state. They will be integral in the effort to help humanity back on its feet.

New ways of living and flourishing on your planet will be taught by all parties involved. Understanding universal laws, and bringing harmony and peace to Earth's survivors will be an important component of our teaching and support. We are teaching you these things so that you might teach others the way to true spiritual enlightenment, and lay the foundations for humanity to regain its footing. Gone will be the days of exploitation, greed, and wars. Peace will reign on Earth as it should be, and new, more plausible systems and ways of living will be taught and shared by many. We, along with others will also gift humanity with new technologies and understanding, utilizing various forces on Earth to bring greater convenience and needed resources into play without jeopardizing the well-being of the planet. Your population will recover, but will never again reach the pinnacle of numbers it once had because such numbers are not sustainable within the delicate ecological balance required by your planet.

We understand that change is not easy for you. You are too addicted to your comforts and distractions, being lulled by the pleasures they give you. Unfortunately, when they are no longer present in your lives, you will have to be strong enough to adapt to what will be very different and less gratifying. You will have to confront your shortcomings and your ignorance. Being numb to your own pain and discomfort will not be an option. Rather, all of you will awaken to those inner conflicts and pain and be encouraged to expiate these conditions buried deep within you. You will be presented with the choice of resolving those inner issues and disharmonies or be given the option to insist on the status quo. Free will reigns in the universe and choice will always be present in any situation you face. Those who refuse to change will perish because they will no longer be able to live in a world that has changed so fundamentally. Those who are resilient, creative, and open will move forward and quickly gain a foothold. You will benefit from the help and support of many enlightened beings who are eager to show you the way forward. We will share technologies and mechanisms that will lighten your burdens but not impose stress on your natural systems. It will be a substantial leap forward for the human race, and soon you will find your place in the intergalactic family of humanity throughout the universe. This will be a tremendous time of healing, enlightenment, and harmony for all those who subscribe to what will be given by the divine source.

We see many events happening within the next decade. The polar icecaps melting at unprecedented rates will continue to accelerate and progress toward total dissolution. Large volumes of CO_2 and methane will continue to be released into your atmosphere accelerated by the Earth's warming. This will quicken the reversal of the last ice age, and in turn accelerate rising global temperatures and ocean levels. Your tropical and subtropical regions will grow quickly, engulfing the world in a climate not seen since dinosaurs roamed the Earth. A new Mesozoic Era is beginning to take shape. It will change the shape of your landmasses radically as low-lying areas will succumb to rising oceans and increased precipitation. Many inhabited areas on your planet will encounter great challenges keeping the oceans out of the cities and farmlands. There will be great hardship for those who inhabit the lowlands. The sea will poison many fertile lands with its salty effluent causing a great deal of hardship and starvation.

As the polar regions and glaciers worldwide melt, new diseases will emerge as pathogens that had been locked long ago in the ice become active once more. Pathogens that will devastate vulnerable populations, and combined with climatic disruptions, will bring world economies to their knees. There won't be one devastating pandemic, but a series of them delivering a catastrophic toll that will cause great fear and chaos.

Plasmic eruptions and solar flares are building in intensity. They will wreak havoc causing your communication systems to be unreliable at best. These pulses of energy will not completely decimate your electrical systems, but will cause severe transmission limitations affecting the world's power grid. Satellite and cell phone communications as well as a myriad of other modalities, will no longer be effective. The military will quickly devise ways of shielding their systems — unfortunately not extending to civilian installations. Much of your commerce dependent on these systems will collapse, bringing financial institutions and flow of financial resources worldwide to a virtual standstill, never again to be resurrected. The way countries and communities do business in the future will be reliant on small-scale local bartering in direct exchange of labor and goods, a reversal of two-hundred years of social and economic development. Governments will remain functioning, but their ability to be effective will be severely limited. Books, rather than electronic means of transferring knowledge, will be the saving grace for humanity. Combined resources with support from bright spirits, star friends, and others like you, Jeremy, will resurrect humanity to be able to flourish and develop into harmonious beings.

Humanity will flourish in harmony and love when the transition is complete. New economies, new forms of spirituality and social organization will be established. The myriad of help and support for you during the transition will teach you new ways after the tumult. Those who survive will gladly listen and implement what is gifted to them by intervening sources motivated by love and care for humanity.

This plan is far-reaching, containing many components working together to realize the ultimate goal of flushing out the dysfunction and disharmony. All of this could have been realized through less painful means, but the inhabitants on Earth require harsh lessons to awaken and realize change.

Lessons will be learned, and many in the population will fall away as physical and spiritual conditions manifest. Those who lose their lives do so out of divine mercy as they will be incapable of living in this new world. It will be a world sustainable and vital — capable of nourishing a renewed humanity, eager to start fresh, and fueled with new ideas infused with a profound understanding of life's purpose and meaning. Those who transition to your spirit world will continue on their journey toward truth in a different way — one unencumbered by physical limitations and restrictions indicative of this plane of existence. In time, all will find their way to light and harmony, whether they encompass physical life or not.

I realize that this is a lot to absorb, Jeremy — both frightening and fantastic at the same time. In time you will heed my words and begin to comprehend their relevance. I urge you not to be frightened or downcast; but rather see what is to take place as a gift. There will be hardship and turmoil in this transitional period, and it cannot be avoided. In the end, you will know great peace, and humanity will know the universal knowledge that is the formula for a good and well-lived life. The progeny of humanity will not know want or fear or hardship. Instead, humanity will be given the ability and resources to sustain and maintain life. These things will be hard won and take their toll, but you will be grateful for the gifts given. This transformation process will draw in many forms of support and love from universal sources. Humanity will receive an abundance of knowledge, material help, and inspiration in order to assist all in reaching the goal of becoming a reformed world capable of sustaining harmony and peace.

Orion then left, leaving Jeremy's desire for facts and details satisfied, but also producing within him a sense of dread for the future. How could anyone survive such disruptions and challenges? With Covid causing a lot of pain and loss a few years back, the idea of the equivalent of multiple assaults on civilization was hard to comprehend. Maybe Sadie will be the lucky one by avoiding those calamities of the future. Oh, how he wished to return to a blissful state of ignorance, oblivious of the future, but it was obvious that this could not happen.

Sadie was spent. The amount of power required to deliver such a harsh message sent her into a tailspin. Combined with her precarious physical condition, she could only think of her bed. So Jeremy escorted her there, feeling his own burdens and deep realization of the grim future ahead. An uprising of grief caught in his throat as the dawning realization came that he would be without Sadie to help him through these looming tough times. What started as a fine day for them both became a downer of extreme proportions. He left without a word as Sadie fell into a deep sleep.

Chapter 26

REVELATIONS

Sadie was lost in her reverie, looking pale but serene as she slowly came out of her trance state. Although the mediumship was not getting harder as she became more ill, coming back from that other place was. It seemed that she was being acclimatized to the next world through these sessions with Orion and Jeremy. And as they delved deeper into their relationship with Orion, she felt less attached to the material world and more to the world of spirit. In the past sessions together, she was often cognizant of his communications, but now they had become a blur, unfathomable, and vague. When she came to, she saw a look of shock and confusion on Jeremy's face. It was as if he had seen a ghost. Sadie knew that she couldn't just leave him and go straight to bed, though she certainly felt like it. She needed to help ease him into a more equitable state before they said their goodbyes for the day.

Slurring and groggy, Sadie asked, "How are you, Jeremy? You look upset."

"I am upset, Sadie, not just because Orion told us some gruesome details of what was to come, but I am beginning to realize that I'm going to have to face these hardships without your strength and wisdom, he said with tears forming around the corners of his eyes. Knowing that you are not long for this world, combined with the knowledge that the present world is not going to last either, it's a bit overwhelming", he said with his eyes blinking rapidly as he stifled back more tears. "This is not at all what I expected when we made our plans with Orion. I thought that we would go on a spiritual magical mystery tour and live happily ever after as our spiritual selves broke free from the weight of earthly life. Well, it appears that you are destined for such a place, and I'm destined to live a life of hell," he exclaimed with frustration and desperation.

Sadie was sobered by his distraught condition. She wondered what Orion had said to upset him so. Surely, he wouldn't have intentionally hurt Jeremy since she knew that Orion was pure love. Yet, whatever he said upset Jeremy thoroughly. Now alert and more present, Sadie asked, "So, you are upset because Orion spelled out what's coming down in the near future?"

"I knew that changes were coming, and Orion hinted as much, but what he described shocked me. It's as if everything we know in life will no longer exist," he said with wide, frightened eyes in his response to Sadie. "Like some terrible end of the world movie that responds to every deep fear we have about the destructive forces of nature unleashed and hell bent on destroying us all.

"Life will never be the same with no way to make a living, and no escape from our frustrations and pain. It seems there will be no pleasures at all, just raw grinding poverty and loss', he lamented as Sadie looked on in deep sympathy for Jeremy's now fully awakened state.

"And you will be released from all of this sometime soon. I envy you Sadie, he said with fierceness that he rarely displayed. You're the lucky one who will escape the pain and retribution that God will put on us for our willful ignorance and recklessness. I'm sure that you will find bliss in heaven while the rest of us rot in hell as the world falls apart before our eyes," grief turning into bitterness and anger.

"Oh Jeremy, Sadie said in a rare moment of pleading despair. If I could live this pain for you, I would. But I have done my time here and God knows why it's time for me to go, but go I must in accordance with divine providence.

"You have no idea of how truly strong you are Jeremy, now regaining her composure and displaying her natural strength and clarity. You have been given all that you need to withstand anything the world can throw at you, she declared with great confidence. It's only your mind that screams in fear and speculation of what is to come. It is crucial that you need to put into practice what you have been taught, Sadie pointing her finger at him for emphasis. Faith, Jeremy, faith is what will carry you through. You have to trust in your inner light and strength while giving up those old habits of fear and mistrust. You must believe that God has a plan for you. How else could all that has happened to you so far have come to pass?

"Yes, the world is about to change, Jeremy, Sadie said with a calmness that emphasized her words. You need to know that you have the capacity to adapt and change with it. What are you most afraid of? Life will go on, and you will go on until your time is up. Nothing will hold you back except yourself from the destiny that you were born with to help usher in a new age. I understand that you are already feeling alone and abandoned, but it isn't true," Sadie asked with all seriousness. "Do you think that after I am gone, Orion will also be out of your life?" "No," she said with deep sincerity, "he will always be by your side. In fact, you really don't need me anymore as the one Orion talks through. While we have been sitting together all these months, they have been developing your own capacity to communicate with both him and our spirit friends. Unaware to you, preparations have been ongoing for some time now. I've seen it and I know it," she said with absolute assurance.

"It was a day of many revelations, both expected and unexpected," Jeremy thought as he regained his composure. As always, Sadie's reflections and perceptions helped center him and add much needed wisdom to his thoughts. The fear left and, in its place, rose up a sense that he could conceivably overcome anything. His thoughts did not come from confusion, but from somewhere deeper and less filled with distortions. He was beginning to know that other part of himself which he was beginning to recognize as his soul — a place yet to be fully known, yet understanding that it was functioning on a different level than conscious thought.

He wanted his soul to have a more conscious role to play in his life. He thought of his childhood and in those days, he was far more attuned to his authentic self than now. He knew this as a state of intuitive knowing and being, something that was a normal experience in childhood, but lost in the harsh reality of growing up. He began to understand that his loneliness as a child was actually a gift; and without time to be attuned to his soul in all its innocence and creativity, reconnecting now would have been far more difficult. The revelations of the moment helped him reach a powerful level of comprehension. It allowed him to see all pieces of his life form a picture of why he was now in a state of readiness for what is to come. As his perceptions shifted, it swept away all doubt, and in its place was the awakening of faculties and gifts that only the soul possessed. A powerful feeling of gratitude rose up deep within him, and he thanked God for his gift of life. He saw how he and God were connected, sharing a powerful plan which he knew was given and absorbed within him long before he was born. He was humbled by the power of it, and he knew that everyone was gifted with some purpose to fulfill. He was not the only player in God's great plan, but rather he was extremely fortunate to know it and be gifted with clear motivation and direction.

Jeremy snapped out of his reverie noticing George the cat purring and gently kneading his chest back to reality. Sadie was nowhere to be seen. He wondered how long he had been out exploring the recesses of his soul. He felt both refreshed and changed. What started out as weeping and whining for what was to come, morphed into joy and peace.

Had Sadie something to do with it, he wondered. Maybe Orion put him in some sort of trance in order to rouse him to this state of soul consciousness. He was unsure, but for now he wouldn't continue to question how and what happened. Rather, he was content to bask in the afterglow.

He got up and looked for Sadie, discovering her fast asleep in her bed. Best not to disturb her, he thought. So he crept out the door and left for home. Rex, as always, was patiently waiting for him in the truck. Rex was especially affectionate with him as he got into the cab, licking his face with abandon. Animals knew their humans' emotions and responded without hesitation. Jeremy's glow was irresistible to Rex, and he connected with him in what was a natural expression of affection. After some cuddles, they headed home with Jeremy humming one of his favorite tunes, *Oh My Sweet Lord* by the Beatles. Rex rested his head on Jeremy's leg, and with the sweetness of the day enveloping him, he thought that life couldn't get any better. In a way, he was right, as the sweetness will inevitably begin to sour as things changed and the world resisted that change.

Chapter 27

FAITH AND FEAR

Everything took on a new hue for Jeremy. He saw his material work as meaningless considering what was coming. Although Orion did not set a timeline for these dramatic events, in his gut Jeremy knew it would be soon. He wanted to warn everyone and shout to the world that everyone needed to prepare for the onslaught of deep earth changes. Yet, he also knew that his efforts would fall on deaf ears as he had seen a worldwide denial of reality as it is. No manner of shouting and cajoling would rouse his fellow man out of their slumbers. They existed under too many layers of ego and thought to force them to wake up and face what was very real. He felt those familiar pangs of loneliness that were so often his fate even though he felt more comfortable and compassionate with himself than ever before. The reality of having few to share this new found truth with anyone other than the Sadie was a cold comfort. He was both lost and found in his emerging reality of soul. "Why does God have to make things so difficult?" he shouted out in utter frustration. He knew that God didn't create these circumstances, and that humanity did it all by themselves. But as one man desperately trying to be in harmony with God, why would he be alone in this struggle? It was not fair or just.

He continued his daily routines, not finding the comfort he once did. Instead, he went through the motions, lacking any life or enthusiasm. His depression got the better of him, and everyone around him sensed his downcast demeanor. Even poor Rex was at a loss to cheer up his master. The best he could do was insisting on walks and attention outside their usual routines. This had a minimal effect on Jeremy, but Rex's love and needs kept him upright and at least partially in the game.

Muriel Phelps was again deeply concerned for him. The poor boy is certainly taking the news of Sadie's imminent demise very hard. She tried to cheer him up with some of her delicious baked goods, but that only brought a brief glimpse of a smile to his face. She acknowledged his pain at tea time and expressed how sorry she was about Sadie; but she felt she was not getting through to him. So she asked if there was anything else that was bothering him.

"Yes, there are a number of things bothering me Muriel," he said with eyes heavy and almost vacant.

"Can you tell me about them?" Muriel inquired with her gentle tone and motherly approach.

"I don't think that you will understand Mrs. Phelps," said Jeremy with the conviction of a man misunderstood and feeling overwhelmed by his fate.

"You can try Jeremy, since I don't intend on going anywhere. We can set aside the entire afternoon if that's what it will take to share your story," said Muriel with firm conviction and compassion.

"It would take at least that long to tell the whole story, but if you insist, I will tell you all that I can." With that, Jeremy laid out Orion's understanding of the fate of their world. He spared no details and the gravitas of his story felt like a leaden weight on the lap of poor Muriel.

She was a bit taken aback by what Jeremy said. It made claims of alien communications from the past mild in comparison to what Jeremy shared on this day. Trying to compose herself, she made a hasty remark which she immediately regretted. "Are you sure that this isn't something that you and Sadie have cooked up together in order to bring some greater meaning into your lives? After all, Sadie is dying and you have little more than this extraordinary event to enrich your life, Jeremy?"

"I honestly wish that you were right. I know how unbelievable all this sounds", he said with a deep sadness. "I certainly questioned everything like you are now, but my questions have been answered in ways that are personal to me — experiences that I can't share right now. If it is proof you need Mrs. Phelps, I have none to give. In time, if what I have said is true, then you will know too."

She cast her eyes downward in regret, offering her apologies for being too quick to judge. How could she believe this fantastic tale since the world didn't seem to be coming to an end? There are certainly troubles in the world, but nothing that requires deep concern or panic. It just seemed the usual machinations of a society churning out both good and bad outcomes in everyday life. Surely Jeremy was mistaken and Orion, whoever he portrayed himself to be, is wrong in his pronunciations of the state and the fate of humanity.

How could she convince him of his grievous errors, and set poor Jeremy back on the straight and narrow? The poor man seemed too far into his funk to be pulled out of it too readily. She was resolved to remain a good friend and listener, rather than preach to him about his misguided thinking, despite her eagerness to do so. They were two people of opposite sides of the fence, wanting to share a friendship but knowing a major breach in trust and understanding had taken place. Feeling in a very awkward dilemma, they covered their tracks by apologizing and backtracking to a tried and true means of communication. Ignoring what had happened between them, each rose from their seats and attended to the tasks at hand with little more than a nod of acceptance that the real world was calling them.

Nothing further was said, but an unuttered agreement of silence remained between them for quite some time. Jeremy felt unburdened by his confession, but Muriel was deeply disturbed by what Jeremy had told her. A pact of silence was the only way either of them knew to maintain respect and care for one another, unfortunately creating a wide chasm between them. They both felt terrible regret and missed their old friendship founded in trust and mutual respect grounded in the practical things of life. She couldn't help but blame herself by introducing Jeremy to Sadie, and by abruptly blurting out her true feelings about what Jeremy had just said. How stupid of me to be so forthrightly honest, she thought. I certainly stuck my foot in my mouth this time, she mused. I'll just have to find a way to patch things up between us. After all, friendships like the one that Jeremy and I have don't come along every day, she thought to herself, feeling a sense of purpose and conviction.

Jeremy felt hurt and more alone than ever by the lack of his friend's endorsement. He trusted Muriel and respected her opinion, but it was a mistake to put her in the position of judging his experiences. What else could she do than to reject something as weird and unique as what had happened to him with Orion and Sadie? How could he possibly convey this knowledge and experience without some sort of context to go with? Muriel was inevitably lost in the weeds the further he went into the story. Her reaction was understandable, he thought as he tended to her rose garden. He was resolved to apologize to her and make amends.

When they met at the end of the day, they both started their apologies at once. A jumble of words fell from their lips, creating a deluge of apologies and requests for forgiveness. They both started to laugh at the comedy of the situation and in that moment, all was forgiven. Muriel vowed to listen more carefully to what Jeremy had to say, and Jeremy was resolved to be a little more circumspect with his sharing. They both went away feeling better and more at peace hoping that in the future, they would find more common ground.

Jeremy knew how odd his story was and what a difficult position he had put Muriel in. He was looking for comfort and acceptance in a world that truly misunderstood his perspective. At that moment, he realized that truth can be a hard thing to swallow. Most people didn't really want to know the truth rather they were content to be ignorant or blind. No wonder the world was going to hell in a hand basket. He began to see how any form of intervention at this point would be futile. He would have to let go of his innate desire to fix things, knowing that there would be some sort of resolution in the future. His part in it was still unclear. He desperately wanted clarity and purpose since he felt that he was holding crucial information that others needed to know and act upon. His sadness turned into a sense of futility. 'Why did Orion give him this information if there was no way of using it? He lamented. There was so much he didn't know and so much he couldn't know. He could only pray and hope for Divine Guidance to resolve his dilemmas. Since faith was becoming a tangible part of his life, he understood that exercising faith in difficult situations was often the only alternative. He understood that life would go on. He couldn't control life or the free will choices of others. All he could do was be in alignment with his Creator and seek guidance. He resolved that he was witnessing the end of an old era and the beginning of a new one. This gave him hope and hope was all he could ask for now.

Chapter 28

ORION'S LAST MESSAGE

It was a clear October day full of the gentle peace that came with a soft dampness in the air and falling leaves littering the ground. The sun, now lower on the horizon, highlighted the fall flowers and brightly colored berries in the landscape. It was the blessing Jeremy needed as he entered Sadie's little cottage. Inside was the disturbing smell of medicine and illness. No matter how many drying herbs Sadie used to hide the smell, it was too strong to be ignored. Sadie's time was close, and they both knew it. Although they hadn't met for a session in a few weeks because of Sadie's illness, he visited her every day and did everything he could to make her comfortable. Today she was determined to have a prayer and session with Orion for at least one more time. Jeremy was filled with both happiness and sadness. He missed those sessions and longed for their return. Today marked a special occasion, and they were both eager to make the best of a difficult situation — eager for Orion to come and join them.

Sadie's cats were unusually restless. They too sensed their world was about to change and not for the better. Sadie always put out special treats to distract her feline friends, ensuring a quiet space for their time with Orion; so Jeremy took on that task for her today. Sadie had lost a lot of weight, causing her skin to sag and deep wrinkles in her usually round and smooth face. Her eyes were sunken and bloodshot — her breathing raspy and labored. Though she had not lost the charm of her forthright nature, it had turned into a stoicism insisting that she remain present and be acknowledged not only by Jeremy, but by her spirit friends as well. She would not be defeated yet. She knew that her time was fast approaching. Now using a walker, she maneuvered it to her usual chair. She started by apologizing to Jeremy for not preparing some food. She was now relying on friends, including Jeremy and Muriel, to do her shopping and food preparation. Her doses of morphine were increasing daily, but today she cut back considerably in anticipation of their time together. Though she was somewhat confused, on the whole she was clear-headed with a bearable level of pain. The fierceness in her eyes was still evident — her voice was steady and determined. The old Sadie remained under the blanket of a barely recognizable shallow layer of herself — all skin and bones, ready to give up the ghost any minute.

Jeremy had never before experienced a death like this close up. The machinations of such a passing sapped both one's dignity and will to live. Each day as Jeremy witnessed Sadie's struggle to stay alive, it brought new horrors and revelations regarding her capacity to withstand the excruciating pain and failures of her body that came. It was a fate you wouldn't wish on your worst enemy, but here before him was his beloved friend undergoing pure torture with her body collapsing under the weight of unbridled cancer cells running amok. His sadness deepened with each day, and there was no way to avoid the obvious as Sadie continued to lose her battle. Sadie insisted on no live-in help; she preferred her privacy instead. She astounded the doctors and healthcare practitioners with her ability to manage alone. They had never met anyone with such tenacity and courage. Sadie knew that it was due to the spiritual help afforded to her from her angel guides that made the difference. Soon she would need someone by her bedside day and night, and she secretly hoped that Jeremy would volunteer for the job. She would have to initiate that conversation with him, but for now she was eager to get on with the task at hand.

Sadie started with a prayer. "Beloved creator, we come to you opening ourselves to universal wisdom and love, all of which emanates from your exalted soul. It is our desire for you to help us toward greater understanding and truth. We seek your blessings in our time of need. We ask in all humility to rain your light and love upon us so that we might know the splendor of the mana from your great soul. Lift us above the confines of this world to a place of grace and peace. Open our awareness, so we may communicate with our dear friend Orion. Please grant us these gifts in the truth of your love. Amen."

The sweetness of Sadie's prayer brought a tear to Jeremy's eye. Oh, how he would miss her prayers — so sincere and eloquent in their heartfelt simplicity, he thought as the atmosphere in the room quickly changed and Orion made his presence.

"Greetings to you my friends, I am grateful that we can spend this precious and needed time together. I am aware that this form of communication is very taxing on this instrument, so I will try to be brief with my comments.

"You have both been dedicated servants to our cause. You have not waivered, nor have you distorted the information given to you. Your loyalty and courage is very much noted by us. Without your dedication and trust in our mutual efforts to reveal universal truth to the world as we understand it, our mission would have been far from successful. There are certainly those on your planet who would have welcomed such an opportunity with open arms. Unfortunately, many of these individuals are steeped in notions and beliefs that would have distorted our efforts greatly, rendering them ineffective. Beloved friends, you have an innate capacity to know what we are trying to convey to you and in time, to the world so there is little distortion. You have both been ideal candidates; and I congratulate you on what has been accomplished so far. Jeremy, you have exceeded our expectations. You have gone far in your pursuit of adopting spiritual truth on the road toward enlightenment. Although there were times when you were ready to reject the mutual contract between us, you always returned to the bosom of our agreement as you discovered and tested the truth. Each time you returned, you were stronger and better informed than before. Sadie has done an admirable job in supplementing our teachings with practical and important lessons for you to absorb. In essence, each and every moment since the beginning has consisted of conscious and subliminal teachings and inspiration. Even while you slept, we were with you, utilizing the receptivity of your sleep state to infuse and clarify truth into your consciousness. You have been well taken care of by a multiplicity of forces, unseen and unrecognized — nonetheless very active in assisting you in your progress.

"Unfortunately, it appears that your time with your beloved cohort is coming to an end. We have made great efforts to ensure that she would stay the course until our lessons were complete. We have indeed given you the basics of universal truth so you might use them to your advantage. There is always more truth to convey, but since you are mere babes in the continuum of spiritual growth and attainment, we cannot give you more than you are able to absorb. We are content with your response to our teachings and we will share more in the future as you are better equipped to integrate that knowledge. As you may wonder how we might accomplish this, it creates uncertainty that will result in fostering continued doubts about your own abilities to communicate with us. Dear Sadie is an ideal conduit that we used to ensure clear communication with you up until now. You have matured a great deal since we began and now you are ready to enter into the next step. We are ready to proceed to another format and level of communication. Our ability to communicate with you telepathically has always been present. How else could I have appeared to you on the mountain? Though in your mind you were convinced that I was there in the flesh, when in truth it was a construct of your mind impressed by our thoughts. Yes, your dear companion saw us as well, but that was because you are both so deeply connected psychically. Consequently, each of you saw what we had intended for you to see.

"The next phase of your development is ready to proceed. The groundwork has been laid, and the interconnections of mind, spirit body, and soul are hardwired to speak with you. You are now ready to test these connections and gain more agility. It will take some getting used to, but you are, in fact, already utilizing these capacities in your daily life. Your recognition of a duel form of consciousness residing within you is proof of it. Your description of the two-world experience is an apt analogy. Few have had this experience, as most of humanity glides along the surface of consciousness rather than delve more deeply within it. In times to come, humanity will learn the truth of their often hidden abilities. There needs to be some who stretch the envelope as you would say, demonstrating their abilities clearly with practical applications. Until your species comes to understand innate and valuable abilities hidden deep within them, how can you truly know who and what you are?

"We intend to enlighten humanity towards knowing their true nature and abilities. We start small with individuals like yourself, but in time and with the right coaching and guidance, your light will enlighten others. Moving forward, the world will light up with understanding, and know a great peace and joy. It is truly a magnificent plan and you, dear Jeremy, were chosen to be enlisted into that plan. Please take comfort in these words, my dear friend. There are always many routes to the same destination. If a roadblock appears, those with wisdom will find another way. Unfortunately, this will be the last transmission through this dear instrument. She has put up a valiant fight, and soon it will be time to release her body to the elements. Her reward will be in gaining a new life in another dimension. It is by no means the end of her as an individual, rather a transformation of consciousness and body to a new plane of existence. She will be freed of the encumbrances of the flesh and come to know great joy in that freedom. You will not lose her, Jeremy, but gain a

STARLIGHTS GLEAMING | 168

much needed ally from a place that you may access at any time. She will be there for you, as will we. As you come to hone your skills in a new form of communication, you will find that we will be very close indeed. We are always ready to assist and support you on what will be a very long and exceedingly interesting path forward.

"Unfortunately, I must leave as I'm afraid that we have overtaxed our instrument. Remember, your dear friend's passing does not mark the end of the journey, rather the transition to a new beginning. You will not be alone Jeremy, instead, you will discover new ways of accessing what you need from your star and angelic friends. It is all a great adventure, is it not? Our hope is that we will talk soon."

With this Orion was no more, as the tired and worn presence of Sadie re-emerged. Oh, how tired she was, though she was glad that they had completed this session. She knew that Orion had set out a plan and that there was no need to fret over her passing into the spirit realms. He had told her as much before the session. Now she was free to go. The job was complete in terms of her involvement with Jeremy who was well on his way.

She hobbled back to her bed with Jeremy's help. She then asked him if he would stay awhile. He was all too happy to comply. They didn't say much, merely quietly comfortable in each other's presence. Soon Sadie fell into a deep sleep — a sleep that she would never awaken from. It took only a few hours for her to pass — a small mercy for them both with her ease of passing, not common with her illness.

Jeremy wept. He was unable to stop the tears; but they were good. He needed to release the grief and tension that had built over the past few months. The struggle was over for Sadie, and she could go home in peace. He felt both deep sadness and a sense of joy for her. He knew that he would keep her in his heart and mind forever. He thought about how extraordinary this relationship was — one that many didn't truly understand or appreciate. It was the highlight of his life so far, something he never would have guessed to happen. Yet it did, in such a peculiar and unusual way that even he had trouble truly understanding what actually took place.

Life goes on, he thought in his bittersweet grief, and he was determined to make the best of it.

Chapter 29

ONE YEAR LATER

The pendulum of Jeremy's mind kept swinging between the revery of truly discovering his soul while worrying about his future, and the future of humanity. Contradictions became obvious as Jeremy took stock of the human condition. Life in Madison wasn't any different from its usual ebb and flow of activities and routines. News of wars, tragedies, and politics had its usual tone of urgency and fear, though nothing was so extreme as to cause widespread alarm. It was business as usual and that business was bleak indeed. The town continued to capitulate to economic forces that shaped its lifestyles and beliefs. Jeremy turned a blind eye to what was going on as he had more pressing concerns to deal with. His clients, family, and friends all went about their business oblivious of their impending fate. Orion's warning of a changing world seemed without substance when he looked around him, but his friend's words continued to echo in his mind about how the world was asleep and humanity would wake up too late to do anything to save it.

Jeremy could only keep a steady course, living his dual life, and compromising between the two realities. In addition to these concerns was the loss of his beloved friend Sadie. His grief still cut like a knife. He had grown reliant on her to help him navigate the two worlds, and now she was gone though he sensed her presence often, dreaming about her almost every night. Her loving presence enveloped him often, like a warm blanket of love and assurance. He knew that she was not truly gone, just present in a different form. Yet, he never felt as alone as he did now. Feeling both deep sadness as well as relief for Sadie, he came to the realization that he had never loved someone as deeply as he loved her. It was a love that abided in his soul, bringing up a bitter-sweet feeling that defined what real love was in the face of loss.

During the progress of his education and transformation from simple mindfulness to soulful consciousness, he gained great insight and understanding into the nature of the universe. Sadie and Orion had given him the keys to the kingdom — not a corporal place, but one that lay within him. That knowledge had shattered his illusions and perceptions about the nature of reality. What he and most people thought to be a reasonable and a deductive understanding of life was completely wrong. Feeling like a stranger in a strange land was becoming a predominant theme in his life. Yet, he still connected with and loved those most important to him. He certainly wasn't about to turn his back on anyone in his life, despite seeing how hopelessly naïve and bogged down they were in the human condition. The world often felt heavy and overburdened by their need for love and fears of rejection. There were many who had no idea how to obtain that love. Jeremy knew the answers to that dilemma, but was stymied by the prospect of how to communicate the message in a way that people could accept. God was a foreign entity in their lives. Formal religion had ensured that God's capacity to love them was severely limited by their beliefs. The common thread on social media was a message of physical perfection, material wealth, and self-empowerment. The pursuit of unconditional love was not part of that journey. He felt compassion for them more than anything. If he understood one thing in his spiritual studies, it is that love was the key to bringing harmony to all things. He was determined to love in a way that reflected this truth. After all, he had lived his life the same as them not that long ago, and in time, he would join everyone in reaping the consequences of a world that is about to be turned upside down.

Working with wood and other worldly things helped to ground him. Experiencing a non-physical reality was part of his daily experiences while engaging in his physical work. Staying in his body with an internal focus was therapeutic. In those times of quiet contemplation, he planned what he would do to align himself with Orion's intended goals. Orion wanted him to practice what he had been taught and to wait. In his mind, it was like watching the fuse of a bomb sizzle and shorten without doing anything about it. He was told to have faith, but that seemed the hardest thing to do right now. He wanted more than anything to save his family and save the world. Yet, he knew that one man couldn't do it all. The best he could hope for was to help convince a few to gravitate toward something more akin to light and life. Since waking up, it became obvious that most people were engaged in destructive and dysfunctional behaviors. He saw that it was not altogether their fault as environment and conditioning had a powerful role —a lack of love in almost every aspect of life caused many to shrivel into a numbed and distorted version of their true selves. Understanding the soul in all its beauty and potential was out of the question when living in such a deprived state. Survival was the goal in a world that constantly challenged and beat people down. The vulnerable child becomes the defended adult, nevermore to seek growth and change as it was far safer to withdraw than to be vulnerable.

Sadie was a contradiction to this approach. She fiercely held her ground no matter what, preferring the company of her feline friends over people. The cats were clear, almost adamant about their preferences. They could be loving and at times cold, but there was no mistaking their intention; and they would be loyal to those they loved. They were themselves at all times while most people barely knew who they were at any time. Sadie followed the road less traveled and paid the price dearly for it. Jeremy would now follow that road, wherever it led, because it affirmed life in its totality rather than offering a distorted version. Although he always felt a little odd, what was now happening was beyond that. It was completely strange, yet there was no better place he would rather be.

Jeremy was true to his word regarding the fate of Sadie's beloved cats. He continued to feed and care for them as he finished fixing up her house.

He intended to live there when everything was in order. His thought was to rent out his present home and move over to Sadie's. That way he was closer to the life that he wanted and a change of scenery was just the ticket. He also had the brilliant idea to transfer the cats to a cat haven nearby. He would donate generously to the cause ensuring their well-being. He kept George, as they had a special bond. The rest, however, were destined to live out their lives with someone who really cared for them. When the deal was done, the lady almost fell over backwards as Jeremy handed her a sizable check.

He never thought that he would appreciate his unusual personality the way he did now. He had acquired a greater perspective from what was truly soul wisdom and perception. He was a changed man — one who could now accept any bizarre and unorthodox experience provided it nourished his soul and mind. Was he ready for what Orion had told him would be coming? Time would tell, but whatever the future brought, he knew that he had friends in high places and a soul ever seeking the divine. If he was meant to survive what was coming, he knew that would be his destiny.

He thought back on that first encounter with Orion up on Mount Edison; and how that day changed everything. Now he was glad of it. His life before was predictable and mundane. He was truly alive and much happier these days. His soul sang its unique song for God's enjoyment. His body moved with renewed purpose and strength. His spirit filled with vitality and light. He realized that the power of love — divine love had opened up a new world for him. If this was what was meant for the world, then he understood why God had a plan. God's plan would unfold despite humanity's blind resistance. It was a plan that would change everything just as it had changed him.

He walked with Rex back up the mountain. It called him now, not in fear but anticipation. For he and Orion often talked together in the shadow of its formidable peak. Rex was now used to this strange man's appearance and smell. The two now conferred with one another about plans yet to be realized and adventures to come. He understood that what the future would bring was dependent on the free will of humanity, yet, alongside humanity's endeavors, was the divine plan which would be undeterred. Like water, it would move around the obstacles set in its path and God would find a way. Of this Jeremy was sure.

Chapter 30

ROMANCE AND NEW BEGINNINGS

Jeremy's life was evolving, and new relationships were in his future. Nickie had come into Jeremy's life through what appeared to be chance. Orion, of course would disagree as he knew that the unseen forces in the world could have a great deal of influence in people's lives.

She was a co-worker with his mother, Judy and during a chance conversation; Nicki mentioned that she was looking for a place to live. Judy thought Jeremy's home would be perfect. Though Jeremy was somewhat reluctant to give up his old home to a stranger, he loved the ample room and acreage that Sadie's home provided. There he could grow all the vegetables and fruit trees that he wanted. Sadie had built up the soil over the years, using compost and free manure from her neighbors. Jeremy had always admired her gardening skills, and enjoyed the delicious home-grown vegetables she added to her cooking. He missed her soups and salads, always fresh and well-seasoned with herbs picked from the garden. Jeremy took on the property partly because of what it offered in amenities, but mostly because it brought him closer to Sadie and their time together. Living here also helped him connect with Orion. Sadie was right in suggesting that he didn't need her to carry on his relationship with the wise old alien. The connection had generously opened almost immediately after Sadie's death. Maintaining a rapport with him in the old farmhouse gave him what he needed now — a firm and comforting hand to guide him through life.

Nickie, like so many, had come from Northern California seeking employment and a better life than the one she had in San Francisco. The timing was right as Jeremy now that he had listed his small bungalow for rent. Nickie loved the carefully tended garden and the cozy feel of the immaculate, older home. Finding this house was a good omen, affirmed her decision to move away from her old life. She immediately liked

Jeremy too. His low-key, almost apologetic, first meeting with her during the viewing of the house left her intrigued, and it piqued her interest. For a middle-aged man, he was not out of shape with some greying around the temples that gave him an air of maturity. He had vitality — one which belied his work life outdoors and a sensible lifestyle. The more she thought about him, the more she felt attracted to him. She wondered if he was gay or divorced, since in their initial conversation, he mentioned that he lived alone. What was a good-looking, nice guy like him doing single in a world full of jerks? Her several bad experiences with those types left her determined to stay away from men altogether. But Jeremy kept popping up in her thoughts which annoyed her. Yet, at least once a week she thought of a reason to call him over to fix some minor problem with the house.

He insisted on maintaining the garden, so when there was nothing inside to attend to, he would pop by after work to water and tend to the garden. She would often invite him in for tea and a bit of conversation when he finished his chores. Jeremy was used to being invited in by his customers, so he would usually accept the offer if he was not too busy. He found out that she liked having dogs around after she mentioned that she was thinking of getting a pet. He finally got up the nerve to ask if Rex could join them inside as they had their tea, and she was agreeable providing Rex with a blanket to lay on and some water.

Jeremy was not a good conversationalist, especially with pretty women. Nickie was not a knockout, but she had a slender, lithe body that made her look ageless. Her long dark hair framed a moon-shaped face set with fiery dark eyes. She had some native heritage on her father's side. He was Cree, and her mother a typical Midwestern farm girl who fell in love with someone her parents felt was the wrong type. This made for problems in the family, so they moved west to California where Nicki was born. In childhood, she felt the sting of people's prejudices. She was often labeled a wetback, though there was no Mexican blood in her veins. Like Jeremy, she spent a lot of time alone as a child, enjoying nature and loving animals. Her first relationship resulted in an unwanted pregnancy at 16, and she was forced to give the baby up for adoption. The boy didn't stick around, and as she pursued subsequent relationships, she was equally disappointed. Now at age 42, her love life was not something she pursued with any interest. She was alone and liked it that way.

Jeremy only saw beauty and grace in Nickie. The attraction made him doubly nervous, though he couldn't resist her invitations to join her. Sometimes she would cook them a meal, often offering Rex a choice bone or a bit of meat. Rex loved her too. It was obvious to him that his master was smitten by her, and that was all Rex needed to be her dog too. For a number of months this casual relationship evolved into something more. Sometimes Jeremy would invite her to his house for a home-cooked meal. Sometimes they would go hiking together, the three of them trudging up Mt. Edison.

Nickie patiently waited for Jeremy to make a move. She was well aware of what another relationship would bring but to her, Jeremy felt different. There was a familiarity that made her feel safe and comfortable with him. No advances were detected in the time they had spent together. She was convinced that he was gay, though he didn't come across that way. Being gay these days was not such a stigma, and there were certainly lots of guys out there which didn't fit the stereotype. She was ok with Jeremy being merely a good friend, but her physical attraction towards him urged her to test her theory.

She invited him and Rex for dinner one Saturday night, making what she discovered was his favorite meal, pot roast with Yorkshire pudding. Though she had never made Yorkshire pudding before, she was determined to give it a try. Because these puffed up delicacies required a hot oven to do their magic, Nicki's oven was capable of the task; but it was also dirty from previous use. Consequently the room filled with smoke, creating a small fire within the chamber, charring the exotic muffins to a burnt crisp. She quickly disposed of the disaster before Jeremy arrived, vowing to never try anything new for a dinner guest in the future.

She wore her best dress — black, low cut and sexy. She set the table with the fine china she inherited from her mother, adding to the table crystal wine glasses and candles. When Jeremy arrived, he smelled smoke and wondered why. He was also taken aback by Nicki's appearance, and the extra effort she put into creating such a nice dinner Thinking that this was a casual invitation like before, he wore his jeans and a t-shirt. Now a little panicked, he thought that he had missed her birthday or some other important occasion. He stammered and stumbled as he greeted her. Inwardly, she found his discomfort entirely amusing, and she wore a slight grin as he went through his apologies. Putting her hand on his shoulder, she calmed him, and replied that there was no need to be embarrassed. She explained that she felt like dressing up tonight and apologized for not giving him fair warning. At this, he visibly relaxed. She poured him a drink and invited him to sit on the sofa.

The room was so familiar to him, although the furniture was different. She had placed her sofa in the same location as he did when he lived there. Thinking of his old home and its comforts, he was suddenly startled to feel the warmth of Nicki's body as she sat down beside him. It wasn't the only seat in the house, so it made no sense to him why she would sit there. He flinched a bit and shifted as far over on the sofa as possible. She gave him a quizzical look, inwardly wondering why he was so reticent.

"Are you OK Jeremy?" she asked with genuine concern.

"Oh, I'm fine he stammered," now flushed and trembling a bit.

He felt like a teenager at his first house party — boys jockeying into position to catch a first kiss or maybe more. He hated these situations, feeling totally out of his depth and too ugly to attract any girl.

Why was he feeling this way with Nickie, he thought as he shifted nervously around in his seat?

I've never told her that I love her because I'm afraid that she wouldn't feel the same. But now I see that she wants to be close. A tingling feeling rose up from his groin and went to his head creating a fight or flight sensation of adrenaline coursing through his body. Feeling discombobulated and tense, he reached out to her with such a reflexive swing of his arm, that he smacked her square in the face.

She screamed in response, putting Jeremy into a tailspin of confusion and regret.

"I'm so, so sorry, he managed to blurt out, his face now crimson red. I didn't mean to hurt you Nickie; I just wanted to put my arm around you."

"Oh, you certainly have a way of expressing your affections Jeremy," as she got up to get a bit of ice to apply to the ugly welt growing on her cheek.

He stepped forward trying to comfort her, this time accidentally kneeing her in the stomach. Nickie let out a gasp as the pain radiated to her neck. She doubled over and Jeremy tried to steady her, unfortunately grabbing her left breast and squeezing hard. Quickly, another expression of indignation came from her lips as she tried to distance herself from him.

Jeremy froze, aware of the ensuing disaster unfolding before his eyes. A sense of mortification crept over him making him ill with unease. He quickly got up, and fled grabbing his shoes and the dog as he exited the door without saying a word. It was the most embarrassing moment of his life, and he couldn't face her as she defended herself from his incredibly bad timing and misdirected gestures. Things could not have gone more wrong, and how could he ever live this down — the thought screaming in his head. He was sure that Nickie would never speak to him again. Quietly sobbing, as he drove home in a fog of disbelief, he contemplated the many other times things went wrong and how he was such an idiot in social situations. What began as a loving gesture from Nickie, turned into such a nightmare. It was proof positive that he was never meant to be in the arms of a woman, but forever destined to be alone.

Nickie was confused. Never before had she been so thoroughly rebuffed by her advances with men. Usually, they were all too pleased to receive her affections, and reciprocated with passion and enthusiasm. Jeremy presented a scenario which she found entirely perplexing. She instinctively knew that he didn't mean to consciously hurt her, but she was also wise enough to realize that the actions of the body often betrayed a truth. Was he so scared of her that he couldn't resist pushing her away? Or, was he such a klutz that this comedy of errors was unavoidable? Rather than being mad, she felt great sympathy for him, and she knew that she had to do something to heal this unfortunate dynamic between them. She vowed to try again to connect. Maybe she needed to wear her old grass hockey gear for protection. But whatever it took, she was willing to take the risk.

She picked up the phone and called him. It took several rings before he answered. Knowing who it was, his voice was plaintive, almost childlike in tone.

"Hello," he ventured, voice squeaking in anxiety.

"Hello Jeremy, she said coming on a bit too strong, trying to counteract his temerity. Are you ok?" she asked.

"It should be me asking if you are ok," he said, now stifled sobs audible over the telephone.

"I'm fine, she said without hesitation. Look Jeremy, I'm sorry for what happened, and I don't blame you for it. It was entirely an accident and I know that you are feeling embarrassed by your behavior. I hope you could come back so we can start over?" she said with a mix of apologies and humility in her voice.

This was entirely unexpected in Jeremy's mind, but her simple words ignited hope in his heart. "Aren't you afraid of me now Nicki? What I did was unforgivable. I don't deserve a second chance. Do I?" his emotions a little less somber, even hinting on joy.

"Of course, I'm not mad at you Jeremy. I know that you wouldn't hurt a fly, but what happened tonight was the result of something else and we need to talk about it face to face. Dinner isn't ruined yet, so please come over and we can patch up this little inadvertent quarrel," Nicki said with urgency. She knew that timing was crucial if they were to make things right again.

She could hear the relief in his voice. He accepted immediately and said he would be right over. He must have driven like a maniac as he was at her door in five minutes. She could see by his bloodshot eyes that he had been crying though they were now bright with a mixture of fear and anticipation, a wild-eyed look that she had never seen in him before. Her relief came as a reflexive move to embrace him. This time Jeremy responded as he should — both in each other's arms coming together in a passionate kiss.

"Oh, this is what I have been waiting for all these months," she said breathlessly as they unlocked their lips.

"Me too, but I didn't know if you felt the same way," he confessed as he dove in for another kiss.

Their dinner remained cold as they headed straight to bed where wild and passionate love-making unraveled their hearts in pure pleasures — lovers finally requited with emotions full in the passion of physical embrace.

Things changed entirely for both Nicki and Jeremy with the events of that night. They talked and talked after their love-making sessions and opened their hearts completely to one another. Unspoken thoughts and feelings that were pent up over the months came pouring out in a litany of confessions and acknowledged fears. With it came such joy and relief as they forged a bond that was to be unshakable for the remainder of their days together — all the while the storms of change were brewing. For the moment, neither of them cared less if the world fell apart. They had each other, and that's all that mattered.

Chapter 31

ALIENS AND ANGELS

It didn't take long for Nicki and Jeremy to set up house together. A few months of back and forth between the two homes blurred into extended stays and then a decision to move in together. The town was abuzz with the events of their new relationship. His old customer and friend, Mrs. Phelps, was ecstatic to hear the news. His mother and sister were relieved and happy to find out that Jeremy finally had a girlfriend. Judy had them for dinner often, and the two women got along famously. Jeremy's sister also liked Nicki, forming a friendship that had its own life.

The world took on a different hue in Jeremy's eyes. He had never known such happiness. His friendship with Sadie and Orion came close, but the love that he was experiencing now was so intense and fulfilling, he almost forgot about Orion and their quest together. He still prayed every day, taking time with God, nourishing his soul with the inflowings of divine love.

Nicki had her own form of spirituality, and it was not diametrically opposed to his. Much of her perspective on life came from the native traditions her father held and shared with her as a child. Seeing the spirit in all life and honoring it was foremost in her spiritual ways. She believed in God, or the Great White Spirit, as her father, George, would say. She had experiences with him that gave her a glimpse into the spirit world, so she was not unfamiliar with that perspective either. George had even mentioned the existence of the star people in their conversations together, but she wasn't sure if they existed, having no proof of her own.

When Nicki and Marilyn were out together doing a bit of shopping and getting a bite to eat, she mentioned to Nicki that she couldn't understand her brother's obsession with aliens. Nicki was surprised to hear about this since he had not mentioned it to her. So she asked for more details; and what Marilyn shared was a revelation. It felt to Nicki like Jeremy was living a secretive life; not one where he was unfaithful, but that he was withholding important information. She felt hurt and a little bewildered, vowing to bring up the subject as soon as possible.

The next morning over coffee, Nickie brought up the subject of Jeremy's extracurricular pursuits. "I heard through Marilyn that you are quite the ET guy, and that you are pretty much into a weird kind of divine love spiritual belief. Why have we never talked about this before? There has certainly been ample opportunity to share your thoughts, Mr. Flynn; so why the secrecy?"

Jeremy was a bit taken aback. He certainly had thought about how he was going to broach the subject, but the distractions of falling in love had taken precedence. He didn't know where to begin, but thought that he should share his bizarre story from the beginning.

"I have a friend who you would have trouble believing is real," he said with almost a whisper. "His name is Orion and he comes from a different planet so far away that no telescope could ever detect it," still with the air of conspiracy in his voice.

"I met him several years ago on Mt. Edison. He scared me to death, but in time we became friends. You've heard my story about Sadie, and you know that she left me this house when she died a year ago. She was a part of this journey too, and we had many conversations with Orion between the three of us. We had set meeting times, and because Sadie had certain gifts, she could bring him through her as if he was in the room. It has been such an extraordinary event in my life that changed me completely." A glow of reverence shone in Jeremy's face, something that scared Nicki a little.

Nickie, as expected, was gob smacked. She had no idea about this peculiar part of Jeremy's life, although she knew that he liked to pray a lot. She was not so close-minded as to write off his story as an impossibility; but she knew it would take a little time to adjust to these new revelations about Jeremy's life. She was quiet and contemplative, not knowing what to say about it.

"I can't get my head around this, Jeremy," she almost choked out the words. "This is almost unbelievable, but your sister had shared a bit with me before this conversation. What you are saying worries me and I'm feeling very confused right now," she said almost coming to tears.

"Oh Nicki, please don't let this be a barrier between us. You can understand why I held back about it because anyone in their right mind would think that I'm crazy." Tears were also filling the corners of his eyes. "It really doesn't change a thing Nickie girl. I'm still the man you, met and will continue to be that person who has integrity and a down-to-earth perspective."

She almost burst out laughing with the irony of his last statement. "You are full of surprises my love, but this one takes the cake. I'm going to have to think about this one for a while before we can go further with this conversation. I love you so much; and I'm willing to adjust to almost anything. But a star man, it's beyond anything I could have imagined," her face now a mixture of incredulity and anger.

Jeremy's sense of anxiety and fear crept up on him as he read her expressions and regretted his words. He was an honest man, and he certainly didn't like to keep secrets, but he knew that letting this cat out of the bag was entering extremely dangerous territory. He had to tread lightly, and gave her a pleading look designed to melt her heart. "I love you Nicki, and I'm willing to give up everything to make things right between us. But, I made a pact with Orion to carry on the work that we began. Its outcomes are unknown right now, and I see no reason to change anything in our life together. I have faith that whatever happens around this issue, we'll still be together. I know that if you let yourself be at peace with this, you will come to see that what I've shared is real; and that you and I will find our way towards mutual acceptance. I want you to know that I can't turn back. I need to continue to pursue my connection with Orion. I feel that the work is just beginning and what is in store for us will be amazing."

Nicki was somewhat disappointed with Jeremy's answers, although in her heart she knew that he wouldn't give something up easily as he was very loyal. The entire scenario was so weird and unbelievable that she wondered if she could ever be a part of it. Communicating with aliens and angels was not beyond her imaginings, but to see herself as a part of that world seemed implausible. For now, she would let it go. Jeremy was right, we were having the best time of our lives; and she wanted it to remain that way. What comes next is anyone's guess. So she backed off, saying that she had a lot to think over and digest.

'You've thrown me a curve ball — something that could change everything, but I hope that it doesn't," she lamented.

"Oh Nicki, my love, you are the number one priority in my life. Nothing will change that. But I want you to be a part of everything that I do — not to have my life carved up in segments pretending that one part is less important than another. I know that I'm a bit strange, yet in my mind everything is coming together in joyful harmony. God was once a stranger to me, but now He is very real and a powerful part of my life. At one time, aliens and angels were the last thing on my mind; but they have become one of the best things in my life. You are far and above that level bringing me the happiness that I never thought I could have; but how does one weigh out these blessings?

"It's all such a fantastic trip — one that has opened my eyes and brought me out of my shell. I have Sadie and Orion to thank for that, and now I have you. Would we have met and fallen in love if I had stayed in my shell never venturing beyond the safety of my routines? We both have God and all the light forces in the universe to thank for what has happened. I hope that one day you will see things in this light. I know that you also have your beliefs and faith in the Creator. My fervent hope, and desire is that we will merge in our beliefs, and forge a strong spiritual connection together. Our physical attraction towards one another is wonderful, but we both know that strong relationships are built on trust and truly knowing each other. I've revealed something that is very personal, and I feel vulnerable sharing this part of me. I can't change who I am, and I don't expect you to change either. But together, we are opening doors to new parts of ourselves. My goal is to develop my soul which is in my true self. I want you to join me in this quest so that we can grow together.

"Life is change, something I never understood until I set out on my spiritual path. I know that love is a constant in the universe along with the love and understanding that we share — and knowing the universe is saturated with God's Love. That healing force can expand our souls forever if we tap into it.

"I know that it's a lot to take in, Nicki but I've given you my inner truth and motivations in a nutshell. It's not difficult or all that confusing. It takes application in prayer, and exercising the soul's longings to be with God. Without this foundational truth, everything that I've said is irrelevant. The path to God is simple and straightforward, and connection in prayer is the key. Asking to receive the essence of God is the most potent truth I know, and it sustains me each and every day. Who taught me this? It was my friends Orion and Sadie."

Nicki's heart melted with Jeremy's words, tears forming and streaming down her cheeks. He was sincerely honest and earnest, and she loved him for it. She would try to understand and maybe even live by what he was saying. It would take time, but they have the rest of their lives to figure things out. She knew that to be her truth.

Chapter 32

TWILIGHTS LAST GLEAMING

It took some time for Nicki to understand Jeremy's perspective. They talked about everything, Jeremy sharing in detail his journey and the experiences he had with Sadie and Orion. They settled into Sadie's old home together, fitting like a glove. Feeling the comfort of the place, and its welcoming vibe gave them a sense that they had always lived there. Even George the cat was pleasant to Nickie, who had a way with animals. The routines of life made for a somewhat unremarkable adjustment as they slipped into one another's rhythms and preferences. They were more compatible than they thought. Jeremy's unusual perspective threw Nicki off a bit. But, as their life together progressed; there was nothing in their approach that caused either of them great friction. They were two peas in a pod; happy to share in the abundance of their love and affection for each other. Rex, George, Jeremy, and Nicki made for one big happy family.

Jeremy shared his spiritual experiences with Nicki, each one more bizarre than the next. Nicki took in his descriptions of traveling to Orion's planet; hearing of what was about to happen to their world, and all manner of metaphysical manifestations that seemed impossible to her. Yet, she trusted Jeremy and knew that he wasn't lying. She had to accept that the world she knew was not Jeremy's world, and who is it to say that hers was the illusion? She began to sit in prayer with him every morning before they went to work. She often felt a lightening of her being as they sat together. Feelings of love for God began to grow seemingly from inside of her. Jeremy explained that her true self was her soul which was deep inside. It explained a lot as her experiences were originating more and more from a place that was not in her head, but rather from her gut. It didn't scare her, but on the contrary; she felt a deep peace and affirmation of self the more she went into prayer with Jeremy. She once had a vision of Orion, his tall slender body looming over her with a big grin on his ample lips. That too didn't frighten her; rather she sensed his love as almost a fatherly thing. As time progressed, she was opening more to Jeremy's perspective. Though in the beginning, she thought that she was under the influence of Jeremy's descriptions and suggestions. Now, however, it felt too real to be a fabrication of her mind. She was beginning to come over to his side of the fence and she felt closer to him than she had ever felt before.

Orion was close too. He continued to utilize the psychic connection that he and Jeremy had built over the years. His communications were always loving and reassuring. It is apparent that Jeremy was meant all along to connect and fall in love with Nicki. She was his soul mate, and even though it took some time and much influence by those who were guiding them both towards their eventual unification, all parties were happy with the outcome.

"Enjoy this time together, Jeremy. As I have told you, these easy days will not last as the world hurtles towards great and dramatic change. You and Nicki will need each other to navigate these changes. Each carries a key to unlock the other's gifts and potential. That opening will be somewhat gradual in the beginning, but as the need arises, the gifts will emerge bringing strength, forbearance, and wisdom to your shared journey," Orion said in his usual authoritative tone — speaking into Jeremy's mind telepathically.

Jeremy didn't want this bliss to end. Disliking Orion's warning, he pushed it down into the recesses of his mind. Yet, he knew that his friend wouldn't lie to him or lead him astray. The world seemed so perfect now with all his needs met in so many ways. "How could the world that I know be in such trouble?" he thought as he was working in Mrs. Phelps rose garden. "I have too much to live for right now," he pleaded as he worked. "Please keep it all going as is until we're ready to pass over into the great beyond." It was the sort of prayer that many before him, and a great many to come have uttered to their Creator. What most did not take into account, was the collective responsibility everyone had to ensure harmony on the planet. There were good people who were aware of this truth, but mostly there were ignorant people completely unaware of their contributions toward an increasingly disharmonious world.

The world outside Madison was not doing as well. Chaos was building as physical changes in the form of weather and geological upheavals intensified daily. There were some countries experiencing these extremes more than others — igniting political tensions as the inequities continued to grow. Extreme variations in the weather caused widespread starvation in the southern hemisphere; while droughts in the north did not allow for any serious assistance towards their southern neighbors. The world was going to hell in a hand basket; though there were pockets of peace and prosperity to be found. Nicki and Jeremy were the lucky ones. They availed themselves of the stability that was part of their region; so it was easy to ignore what was happening elsewhere.

For now, Nickie and Jeremy sustained by their love for one another and were safe. The storm was not yet upon them. They both went about their life with a business as usual attitude. Nothing was further from the truth as the dark clouds gathered; but like so many whose lives were going well, there was no true concern for the future. They both savored life to the fullest even though in the back of Jeremy's mind, Orion's warning was lingering. For now, the sun was shining, the birds chirping, and the garden was rich for the harvest — contradicting Orion's message. Nicki and Jeremy would hold on to the sweetness of life until the very last moment.

— THE END —

REVIEW

"I found this story to be an unexpectedly refreshing source of spiritual insight coming from an unusual source in an atypical way. In a world where there are powerful forces doing their best to convince us that people from other planets constitute a threat to human life and freedom, in this story we have someone from another planet who was invited to help us, humbly shares wisdom, honor's people's choices, and comes here in a gentle way that most people would not expect.

It's rare to see in any work of fiction to see the commingling of so many different and diverse beings, much less seeing them working together in harmony.

While it's clear that this is a work of fiction, it's one that is believably unbelievable to me. Mr. Fike brings the fantastic into the flow of workaday existence in such an unusual, yet believable way. He has written a story describing great difficulties on the horizon where hope and help to match may be available. It is not a story of doom and gloom regarding our future but offers possibilities of what may constitute viable solutions for a weary planet. It is a great read that captures the imagination.

—Margaret Terry Adler, Social Worker and Art Therapist

Excerpts from Book Two

The adventure continues in book two as Orion's visions of the coming earth changes begin to unfold with startling accuracy. In an instant, the familiar world is upended; and what was once a simple, comfortable life for Nicki and Jeremy becomes a daily struggle for survival. Amid this profound transition, Orion offers deep insights into the reasons behind the planet's transformation — guiding them through the chaos with wisdom and unwavering support.

Although life will never return to what it once was, unexpected encounters with both extraterrestrial visitors and angelic helpers shape their journey in remarkable ways. As Nicki and Jeremy face trials that test their courage and faith, each challenge becomes a meaningful lesson. Through it all, their love strengthens into a powerful partnership — one that ultimately helps guide many wounded souls toward a deeper understanding of life's true purpose.

Book Two - Chapter One
JEREMY AND NICKI

For the last ten years Jeremy and Nicki led an idyllic life despite the turmoil of a world reeling in chaos. As Orion had predicted, floods, famine, disease, and political upheavals continued to accelerate with intensity and frequency. Yet, in the quiet town of Madison, life appeared unaffected by these challenges. The town still maintained its charm and stable economy. People continued to enjoy their comforts without too much inconvenience. The town railed with its fundamentally liberal ideology against the rising political perspective of the far right. The people held steadfast, but grumbled about the changes imposed by a federal government, determined to retool the system toward a philosophy of every man for themselves.

Jeremy often thought of his time with Sadie and Orion. He regaled Nicki with experiences and memories of their time together. Nicki grew to appreciate the wisdom that Orion had shared with her mate, and she often joined him in prayer — an important part of his morning routine. She was not as keen as Jeremy yet, but she sensed the goodness in him. They seemingly lived a charmed life, both with stable employment. She taught at the local elementary school while Jeremy continued building his business. They had no debts and were able to take a few fun trips during her breaks from school. Rex was as spry as ever. Blue Healers are known for their longevity and Rex, at age 13 didn't seem to be slowing down. Jeremy, with Nicki's help, had extensively remodeled Sadie's run-down home and garden, making every bit a paradise both inside and out. The new kitchen was the centerpiece of the home with all new appliances and a large space for Jeremy to explore his culinary creativity. Jeremy had also built an add-on to the house for Nicki's own special room to quilt and sew.

The garden was a wonder to behold. New flower beds were dug and artfully developed into a gardener's dream of perennials, roses, and shrubs. There was a sizable patio added to the west side of the house covered by a trellis, draped with several varieties of grapes. The vegetable garden was almost an acre in size, producing far more than they could eat. They both learned how to can, adding so much food to their larder that trips to the supermarket were rare. Fruit trees of every possible variety completed the picture. Their level of self-sufficiency was impressive. Although it took a lot of time and effort, they were happy with their accomplishments and new home, appreciating a simple and quiet life.

Orion had talked about the frog in the pot scenario — enjoying the warm water, oblivious of impending death by scalding. Much of the world was in a similar state of naïve acquiescence. Despite the warnings and signs that all was not well, most preferred to be content in their apathy. Teetering on the edge, like a game of Jenga, each fundamental piece holding up the tower of human endeavor was weakening. Eroded by the cataclysms of earth changes and political instability, how soon it would topple was anyone's guess. It was clear, however, that humanity was closer to catastrophic failure with each day that passed. Life's routines carried on regardless, and Jeremy and Nickie were like everyone else, living day by day without too much thought for the future. Little did they know that they were in imminent danger; nor would they ever have imagined what was coming. If they had known of a realization that life was about to change irrevocably, it would have cut like a knife.

Book Two - Chapter Two
THE BEGINNING OF THE END

It was a beautiful spring day in April, and Jeremy loved to see the garden come alive at this time of year. The warming sun coaxed the fruit trees into full bloom, and the perennials were rising from the warming ground with a vitality and promise that excited both Nicki and Jeremy. The air was sweet with the scent of alder trees blooming as the forest awakened. Warmth had returned to the valley, signaling the beginning of another year of life.

That day Jeremy was out tilling the vegetable garden, getting ready to plant. Rex was alongside him, occasionally barking at the whining machine which harassed them both. "Heal Rex, heal," Jeremy shouted in frustration. But Rex didn't heal as his master commanded, and the dance continued. Rex's ears were filled with the screeching, and he desperately wanted to be elsewhere. His instincts, however, were to protect his master from this strange beast, and it was more important than his own comfort.

All of a sudden, something new and intense filled his senses. It started with a flash of blue light, much brighter than the sky and piercing his brain like a knife. It stopped Rex in his tracks, causing him to give a yelp of pain which his master could not hear over the racket of the rototiller. Then came a roar, so loud it ignited a desire to flee. Thinking the machine was about to attack him, he crouched down taking an instinctive stance of fight or flight. He looked around in anguish and confusion as the noise got louder, but no attack happened. Suddenly, the earth itself started to move in undulating motions that swept both Rex and Jeremy off their feet. Jeremy was at first stunned by this bizarre turn of events; but the roar of the earthquake insisted that he return to his senses. His first thought was of Nicki, who was at school at this hour. He had to get to her, but there was no way of moving in this frightening situation.

It was several minutes before the shaking stopped. Jeremy wondered if the house was still standing. He ran down the path towards the house, praying that it was. The house looked as if nothing had happened. He knew that looks could be deceiving, yet here stood his abode intact and silent after the chaos of what had just occurred. He tried the front door. It was jammed, but he managed to open it. He first saw a jagged crack in the ceiling of the living room that disappeared behind the wall separating it from the kitchen. The wooden cabinet full of old country rose fine china that Nicki inherited from her grandmother had toppled and the dishes were in pieces. He progressed to the kitchen, only to discover that the refrigerator had fallen over, spewing its contents on the way. Cutlery, pots, and pans and most of kitchen ware were strewn over the floor. It was a mess; but no major damage done. He then proceeded to the bedroom to see that the armoire had also fallen over, taking out a portion of the headboard with it. The bathroom was fully intact. Thankfully, there wasn't any water spewing from broken pipes. Jeremy held his breath thinking that maybe the gas line had been severed. He rushed out of the house slipping on a picture that had fallen off the wall in the living room, but caught himself as he slid forward and gained his composure. He flew out the door, and around to the back of the house viewing the intake and gas meter still intact and no smell of gas. He made an audible sigh of relief.

He wondered where the keys for the truck were; once again feeling the panic of having to find Nicki. He forced himself to remember that all the keys were on a hook by the front door. Amazingly, not one had fallen off. He grabbed what he needed and ran for the truck. He and Rex jumped in and headed towards town.

The gravel driveway leading to the main road looked fine — no cracks or fissures. Once he got to the main road, it was a different story. The dirt and gravel had settled easily after the shaking, but the pavement was not so lucky. Jeremy he looked down the road and could only see it in pieces where it was once straight. It appeared like an epileptic snake, writhing in concert with the forces that created it. The road seemed impassable with trees and branches littering the jagged pavement.

Jeremy needed to rethink his strategy. He wondered whether he would go by foot, but speculated that if Nicki or others were injured, he would need the truck for transport. He decided to return to the house and grab some tools from the shed. He took two chain saws, a gas can, oil, pick, shovel, and a come along to move heavier objects.

As he headed down the road into town, he saw smoke rising from that direction. This only created more anxiety and worry with his attempts to reach Nicki. There were others now on the road, having the same intention to reach town and connect with loved ones. They were all country people like him and well-equipped to confront the situation. They all worked together to clear the road. Jeremy's normal five-minute drive took two hours of slogging through debris and obstructions. By the time they got to town, many of the grand old mansions, a proud symbol of Madison, were in flames.

People were yelling and screaming with chaos everywhere. The fire trucks were helpless to move due to the toppled ancient chestnut trees lining the streets, making the road all but impassable. Jeremy tried to flag down some of the parents that were running away from the flames with their children to find out if the school was still standing.

"Some of it is on fire," the anxious mother blurted out. Jeremy was galvanized by her warning and ran the remaining mile to the school. He passed people with injuries asking for help. Some folks were bleeding profusely from head wounds, and more had broken limbs. He couldn't stop until he knew Nicki was safe, and started sprinting faster, dodging fallen trees and wrecked cars. At times, the flames were so intense that he had to navigate his way around them. The grand old homes (the ladies of Madison) were all on fire, marking a tragic end of an era.

What seemed like hours, but in truth were only minutes, he saw the school. The old building was built in the early 1900's, and it was fully engulfed in flames. Crowds gathered around, confused and disoriented, not knowing what to do while witnessing the tragedy of the old school burning its way towards cinder and ashes. He desperately looked for Nicki. Looking at such a disturbing scene made it hard to get his bearings. Once oriented, he saw each face as he quickly strode through the crowd. He recognized a few teachers from the school and asked them if they had seen Nicki. All but one had said that they hadn't. Rachel Hadley, a teacher whose classroom was next to Nicki's, said that she had seen her moments ago going back into the school to see if there were any stragglers. Jeremy's heart dropped as he assessed the state of the fire. He was determined to go in after her, but as he lunged forward, a few men caught him and held on.

"You can't go in there bud," one guy said. "The fire is too advanced and you won't make it out again."

Jeremy was desperate and fought like a madman. "Nicki's in there," he screamed. "I'm going in no matter what," he said with a plaintive, high-pitched voice.

"Oh no you're not," said the second man, "it's a death sentence if you do."

BOOKS FROM THE AUTHOR

Albert J. Fike

THE QUIET REVOLUTION OF THE SOUL: EXPLORATIONS IN DIVINE LOVE
4.7 out of 5 stars (22) | Amazon Paperback, Kindle eBook

The soul is a subject that tends not to get much press, and when it does, many commentators frankly do not know the difference between the soul, the mind, the spirit energy and a human being. So its really great to have a commentary from someone who knows these differences, and knows the differences because of a personal journey of soul transformation. In other words, he is talking from experience.

We are supposed to grow our souls here on Earth, but unfortunately, far too many teachers claim that all we have to do is remember who we are. Sadly that is not the truth. The truth is that we have to do the hard yards. And there is a choice here, we can do the very hard yards or the shorter, somewhat hard yards. The choice is whether we ask God to help in this soul transformation or whether we walk alone. A classic illustration of this harder choice is Buddhism, but it's nearly impossible to find a coherent explanation of how we walk this easier path God-Assisted. This is such a book. Read it closely, and put into practice what it recommends. You will also experience soul transformation, as I have indeed done. It's not an overnight thing, but if you look back on ten or fifteen years of soul growth, you will be amazed.

OUR WORLD IN TRANSITION, MESSAGES FROM JESUS
4.7 out of 5 stars (44) | Audiobook, Paperback, Kindle eBook, Audible

Change is coming to our world. A change so profound and powerful that every one of us needs to prepare for what is coming. This book, essentially written by Jesus through the mediumship of Albert J. Fike, is part prophesy and part spiritual teachings. Twenty lessons received over a six month period take us on a journey of understanding our true nature and the potential to forge a personal relationship with our Creator. Jesus teaches that without greater knowledge and clear understanding of deeper spiritual truth that humanity will suffer through these times of difficult transitions. He speaks of the power of love to heal us all and points to avenues of vast untapped resources that will assist in transforming ourselves and our world. A new world of spiritual and material harmony is coming as the old world crumbles and a new one emerges.

FINDING OUR WAY HOME, BY ALBERT J. FIKE
4.8 out of 5 stars (30) | Audiobook, Paperback, Kindle eBook, Audible

Finding Our Way Home is a continuation of the publication, *Our World In Transition, Messages From Jesus.* Jesus continues to share spiritual lessons designed to awaken our deeper selves and make sense of an ever-changing world. He talks about the power of love to change the hearts and minds of humanity. He continues to speak of a faltering world which, in time, will make way for something completely different and new. He shares his vision of what that world would look like and how Celestial, stellar and other Divine forces work together to help birth a new way for humanity. The depth and breadth of Jesus's teachings and revelations continue to awaken both the mind and the soul in clear and understandable language and concepts, adding to his previous lessons. Another must-read for those who are intent on understanding what is happening in our modern world and how we might find our way to the new and harmonious world to come.

AWAKENING TO SOUL CONSCIOUSNESS, BY ALBERT J. FIKE
4.9 out of 5 stars (10) | Amazon Paperbook, Kindle eBook

This marks the conclusion of a trilogy of books containing spiritual lessons channeled through the mediumship of Albert J. Fike, authored by the Master of the Celestial heavens, Jesus of Nazareth. A journey that is extraordinarily in scope and depth as he shares his wisdom in the form of inspiring revelations designed to awaken our hearts to God's Love. His writing shatters many long-held beliefs about life's purpose and meaning, bringing answers that are simple, yet saturated in truth. Taking us on a path designed to open the way toward liberation, discovering pure and lasting joy with the awakening of the soul.

DIVINE LOVE MEDIUMSHIP, BY ALBERT J. FIKE
5 out of 5 stars 5) | Amazon Paperbook

Since the inspired work of James E. Padgett who brought through the truths of Divine Love with his gift of automatic writing, many have taken a keen interest in the subject of mediumship. Though there has been some information given to us by Celestial Spirit Guides on what Divine Love mediumship is about, a comprehensive book has not been written until now. Albert J Fike, a Divine Love medium himself, has now written another compelling addition in the series 'Explorations in Divine Love'. It addresses many questions relating to this subject. This book is short and easy to read. It is designed to both educate and inspire the reader. It is not just an instructional book for those who wish to become a medium,

AUTHOR

Albert J. Fike is a retired landscape gardener living on the west coast of Canada. He and his wife Jeanne of 50 years have dedicated their lives and travels to educate others on the benefits of prayer for Divine Love. Together, they have traveled extensively, sponsoring retreats, lectures, and workshops on the subject through their organization, Divine Love Sanctuary Foundation.

Al has put his writing skills to work, publishing a number of books pertaining to the development of the soul. He is also a spirit medium who has brought through over three thousand messages from Celestials and other spirits.

His books reflect the information shared through his channelings. Starlights Gleaming, The Story of Jeremy Flynn is his latest effort and first foray into writing fiction. It is an intriguing book about one man's struggles to integrate spiritual truth into his life.